The Art of Losing

By

Mary Pagones

The Fortune's Fool Series

Also by the Author

As Quinn Wilde

For my Academically Talented (AT) teacher Mrs. Prout, who first introduced me to poetry, ruining me for life

The art of losing isn't hard to master;
so many things seem filled with the intent
to be lost that their loss is no disaster.
—Elizabeth Bishop, "One Art"

Chapter 1
Lose Something Every Day

One way to categorize equestrians is by discipline. Like hunters, jumpers, dressage riders, eventers, barrel racers, and so on. A simpler way is by the rider's fears, because with fear, there are only two types of riders. One type fears the horse; the other type fears looking like an ass while riding the horse. I, Simon O' Shaughnessy, am in the second category.

I compete professionally in a sport known as eventing. It comprises three phases: dressage, cross-country jumping, and what you might know as showjumping, but which eventers call stadium. It's because of that latter phase I met Lena Roberts. In some other disciplines, like show hunters and jumpers, your trainer is your guru, your high priest. Eventers are more pagan in their worship. Like a lot of professional eventers, I have diverse trainers for the different phases. I need all the help I can get with my current upper-level horse Morrissey, especially in the stadium phase.

Whether you call it stadium or showjumping or just jumping colored sticks, that phase brings out the second kind of fear in me. Fear of humiliation.

The terrible thing about the fear of being shamed is that it gets worse, the better you get. The more you say, "I'm a professional horseman, and all I know or care about is horses," the more you need to look like you know what you're doing to preserve some sense of self-respect.

Embarrassingly enough, as a kid, I used to compete in showjumping before I switched disciplines. Jumping over those candy cane-colored poles on my fragile, prancing little mare Damsel, no one could beat me. Of course, that local circuit of schooling shows was no A-circuit. But the fond memories linger.

What makes a great eventing horse differs from what makes a great showjumper. A good eventing horse will gallop and jump fast and flat to conserve his energy, and have decent opinions about striding and pace. He'll know when to save his rider, and know when to listen.

Showjumping favors horses with an energy-wasting pop over each fence of the course to ensure a clear round, and a horse which obediently listens to his rider over a manufactured, twisty course that would never exist in nature.

All of this explains why Morrissey—my chestnut Thoroughbred gelding and cross-country machine—and I are so terrible in the stadium phase. I'm trying to make myself feel better by reciting facts, when the only facts that matter to me are wins and losses.

Although my career as a teenager showjumper was ages ago, I shouldn't be this bad. Well, not bad, because Morrissey and I won our last horse trial. Bad by the uncompromising standards of the sport and my own inflexible personal sensibilities that demand perfection in all three phases. I aspire to the five-star level at Kentucky, Maryland, Badminton, and Burghley.

No upper-level eventing rider worth a fancy Himalayan salt lick should lose a competition in the showjumping phase. It's one thing for a horse to dump your ass on the ground going over a solid cross-country obstacle. There's no guts and glory in dropping a pole in the arena, as far as an eventer is concerned. Eventing showjumping is comparatively easy.

Traditionally, the stadium jumps were just there to show the rider hadn't unnecessarily tired out his horse during the real meat of the cross-country phase. Now, sometimes the stadium is before cross-country, to make sure people have enough skills to make it over jumps at all before they're unleashed onto non-frangible obstacles.

Things are always changing in the sport. But one unchanged thing is my opinionated Storm Cat-line chestnut gelding knows stadium jumps can fall down and aren't worth his effort. Enter showjumper Vince Adler, to convince him they are. It's mainly because of Vince that Morrissey and I have improved in our rankings. Vince is honest, has a sense of humor (although not as sweary as mine), and isn't fond of quick fixes to manage bad horse decisions.

I'd always gotten along with Vince Adler's working student, Lena Roberts. She recently aged out of the juniors and went pro. Lena exhibits grit I seldom see in most A-circuit riders. She kept showjumping her last horse—a cheeky bay gelding named Pilot who always pinned his ears back—long after her last trainer told her to get rid of him. It's why she gravitated to Vince. He let her stick it out with the horse.

I admire riders toughing it out with unpredictable, quirky horses. My belief has always been giving up on a horse is like giving up on yourself.

But sometimes that mentality can really bite a rider in the ass. We all cheer when riders defy good sense and stick it out with the rank ones when they're successful. But we try to forget when our unwillingness to have tough conversations about unhappy horses results in injury or worse. I admit, one rainy day at the barn when I was sitting and watching a livestreamed Grand Prix on my phone, when I saw Lena on her gelding Pilot, even I clutched my pearls, if the buttons on my polo shirt counts as pearls.

Lena's horse spooked at the first fence. She calmly circled Pilot after giving him a firm smack of her crop, but he sucked back over the second and the third. The fourth, he went straight through with wild and reckless abandon, flipping over in the mess he'd created, leaving Lena in a pile of poles and legs.

I called her later, not even sure she'd answer. "That looked bad," I'd said.

"I'm fine." Lena's voice had a quiet, reassuring quality that troubled me. When I saw her next, she was on crutches.

"I thought you were fine."

"I had to buy a new helmet. But I'm fine."

"The limp is what, a pirate costume or something?"

"It's not broken! Only a stress fracture in my femoral neck or something. Who has even heard of, or even really needs, a femoral neck?"

Lena sounded brave and made the effort all working students make in such situations—cleaning tack, trying to hop and pick stalls—but it just didn't happen. She had to bow out. Though Lena healed, Vince couldn't exactly kick the new woman out he hired to replace her. Lena moved back to her mom's Maryland suburban apartment. Her family comes from this area, which is another reason she gravitated to Vince's.

Worse yet, Lena's horse had a suspensory injury, so Lena sold him "to a dressage home, riding on the flat only." If there was ever a horse determined to send himself into early dressage semi-retirement, Pilot was that horse. He couldn't have planned it better.

On yet another rainy day, similar to when I saw her spill on the livestream, I was thinking (a dangerous pursuit for any man, but especially one who rides dangerous animals for a living), I hadn't seen Lena riding in a long time. I called her.

"Still hopping?"

"I've quit."

"I know you're out of a working student job."

"I mean, I've quit riding."

"Like, as a pro?"

"Like, I'm studying for my SATs right now. Simon, I've lost my nerve. For the first time since I was on a pony."

"Lost your nerve for competing or riding entirely?"

"Riding's just not fun for me anymore. If it's not fun for me, it's not fun for the horse. I'm always thinking of what might go wrong on a horse, lately, rather than what might go right. I never used to be this way."

That sentence summed up every crappy round I had on Morrissey. I have to shut down those feelings inside Lena and in myself. Lena's a talented, brave, and sympathetic rider. I can't leave her like this. With an SAT book and fear of the future in her weird horse girl heart.

"I have a horse for you," I say.

"I'm not in the market for a horse. Especially an eventing horse!"

"I meant just hacking out. I need someone to ride Owen tomorrow at the horse park. My barn manager, Molly, is shopping for wedding dresses. She rides him all the time." Though Molly isn't getting married for more than a year, finding a dress is apparently a long and convoluted process involving *princess necklines* and *eggshell tulle* and *empire waists* and other phrases I'm trying not to learn.

"Molly is an eventer. I'm not. Simon, it's been forever and a day since I jumped outside of a ring."

"I saw you hacking around Vince's all the time."

"Yes, just hacking. Not riding over solid jumps like you do cross-country. Those jumps don't fall down out there! The fall Pilot took, well, if it had been over a solid obstacle, it could have…"

"I know," I say. I know all too well and intimately the risks of eventing. I don't say *I* wouldn't have ridden unpredictable, reckless Pilot over solid jumps. Morrissey can be an ass, but he's got a sense of self-preservation, even when he's letting his rider fend for himself.

Instead, I switch strategies. "Think of how jumping a little cross-country course on a schoolmaster like Owen will boost your confidence. Besides, it's just for fun. It's not your day job or discipline. We'll be jumping what will seem like tiny toys to you as a showjumper. LEGO-size jumps."

"Have you ever stepped on a LEGO?"

"You know what they say? When a bad horse takes away your nerve, it takes a good horse to bring it back."

"Pilot wasn't bad! He was just sensitive."

Silence.

"Like an artist."

I remain silent.

"Okay, overly sensitive," she says.

I pounce. "Well, Owen is not!"

Owen Meaney (I swear, his first owner named the horse after some book I've never even read, he's not really mean) is an upper-level horse I'm currently trying to sell as the perfect mount for a rider looking to step up from Preliminary to Intermediate. I was planning on campaigning Owen myself. Then it became clear he wouldn't have the scope or soundness to run at Advanced for any length of time. He's a powerful, brave jumper. I trust him.

My trust in humans is harder to win. Like, my boyfriend Eric and I are kind of in a *serious but not serious* yellow zone. I'm alone, yet not alone, for the first time in my adult life. Eric lives with his parents while he's saving up for an apartment and paying off the last of his student loans. He sometimes sleeps over, spending the night with me, sharing a hasty, sleepy breakfast.

When I'm alone in my house because Eric's not staying over or at a school activity, I miss not having someone to bounce my thoughts and personality against, like a hyperactive kid with a red rubber ball and no wall. Other times, I get frustrated having to explain why I make bad choices daily, like eating sugary cereal for energy or scrolling on my phone with my non-dominant right hand when leading a hot horse.

Or not getting up early enough to go on a run. Today, I am greeted by the sight of a showered Eric, sporting a shirt and tie, reading texts at my kitchen table, decompressing after his usual five or six slow miles at dawn. He seems surprised at the sight of me, nearly dropping his phone into his Honey Nut Cheerios, like he was doing a guilty thing.

"I tried to wake you," he says.

Ah, now I remember. I've been trying to run with my boyfriend in the mornings after he sleeps over. But this morning, I ignored his poking, rolled myself into a pill shape, and went back to sleep. He knows I feel less tightly wound when I exercise in the morning; I know I feel less stressed when I exercise before I ride. But I still didn't do it.

Eric has run a marathon, even tried training for an ultra. He's not naturally competitive like I am. He didn't mind coming in last in his age group. When he runs, it's often in an aimless, ambling sort of way. He doesn't take sports seriously. The things he has put his heart into—drama, music—have no clear winners or losers.

I tell him my grand plan for Lena at the horse park.

"Are you sure letting her ride Owen is a good idea to build back her confidence? I thought you said Owen was a pretty powerful horse." He cleans his glasses on a paper towel, which is what passes for napkins at my house.

I rattle peanut butter-flavored Cap'n Crunch into my bowl. Nostalgia kid food I'd picked up on sale at the supermarket. RIP to the roof of my mouth. I know it's not good for me; I know it won't satisfy my hunger like a glob of peanut butter slathered on some grainy whole wheat bread. My teeth have been bothering me, particularly my molars in the back of my mouth. I'm hoping the sugary crackling will distract me from the sensation.

Anyway, I've kept my gangly, freckled frame lean with the Horse World Diet of not eating when horses have needs, and snarfing down whatever junk food I have on hand when there's a break in riding, managing client tantrums, and preventing horses from killing themselves. I see no reason to stop.

Eric is shorter than me, muscular from running, but he has to work to keep himself in shape. Although I do like that shape. I like just about everything about him, except for one key characteristic. "Any horse is too strong for you. You don't even like horses!"

"That's not fair, Simon. I'm afraid of horses. There's a big difference between being afraid of and not liking." He leans back in his chair, brushes his too-long bangs off of his glasses.

"I know horses, and I know what I'm doing," I say and bite down hard on the cereal, which makes so much noise in my ears, I drown Eric's words. Horses are the one thing I know, and if I'm wrong about horses I've known as long as Owen, I don't know myself.

"I just don't understand why you'd put someone who has had a terrible fright on Owen. He's so powerful."

"Owen seems like an intimidating horse *to you*, Eric. Not to a rider like Lena. She doesn't need a pony ride. I can trust Owen to jump whatever he's pointed at, like a machine. Lena's not afraid of speed. She's afraid of a horse refusing and spooking like her old nutter."

"Well, like one of your horses, I must bolt." Eric is teaching summer school at St. Augustine's prep. At most normal schools, summer school is for kids who legit fail a class or refuse to bring a change of clothes for gym. Ironically, I received a D in PE for doing just that for a semester and nearly had to do summer school, although I kind of liked gym (just not the dumb jocks I had to play basketball with or wearing sweats and sneakers rather than boots and jeans to play in). Concerns about missing summer barn time was the only reason I finally stuffed a pair of ratty Converse with pen-and-ink doodles all over them and some shorts in my locker.

St. Augustine's offers enrichment classes for kids who want to take additional AP tests or prep for the SAT or ACT. Kids who say, *summer, who needs that, I'd like more school.* Or who are too weak to defy their parents.

Eric stares at the refrigerator, then makes a peanut butter and jelly sandwich to take with him. Idly, I pick up his cellphone, which is an older iPhone model than mine. He whirls around, butter knife in hand. "Simon! That's private."

I put down the phone.

"I'm sorry, Simon. I didn't mean to react like that, but I'm a teacher. Students send me some texts meant only for my eyes."

"It's okay," I say. I know Eric is the faculty advisor of the Gay-Straight Alliance at his Catholic school, and fought very hard to get the club started. I get some texts from kids are very private. But my last boyfriend left me, the one before that cheated on me, and I cheated on the one before that, so the hair on my neck prickles slightly at the violence of his emotions. I'm suspicious with both the sensitivity of the previously wronged and the guilty.

There are many innocent reasons for Eric not wanting me to see his texts. To stop thinking about ones that aren't so innocent, I rush through the rest of my breakfast and head to the barn to meet Lena.

I've been in the horse business for a long time, which itself some civilians might say is evidence of my poor judgment. But it's kind of crazy, even to me, that Lena was making her way as a working student before her accident, trading labor for free board for her horse and lessons for herself. Only in the sport of showjumping would the daughter of Serena St. Claire—yes, *that* Serena St. Claire, the star of the long-running daytime soap *Riverview General*—be begging, borrowing, and cleaning tack to ride at a competitive showjumping barn.

In the showjumping world, you need to have so much money, money doesn't matter. Enough money to have money making money for your money while you sleep. Having grown up for even a short time as a poor horse kid, with a single, recently divorced struggling mom, I understand all too well that the less money you have in the horse world, the more things cost. In time, sweat, functioning joints, and sanity.

I never watch daytime soaps. But when I mentioned, after trailering back from one of my lessons with Vince, that I'd made friends with Serena St. Claire's daughter, my barn manager Molly was ecstatic. "Oh my God, I used to watch *Riverview General* whenever I was home sick and it was always on the tack room television at the barn where I worked as a kid. My aunt still watches it." She recounted the plots of a number of episodes in detail, which I kind of hate (unless it's a science fiction show), and I tuned her out until she was done.

"I guess I'm not giving you enough to do, if you have time veg in front of soaps," I'd said to Molly, only half-joking. Before the whole wedding thing really got fired up, Molly was one of the most conscientious workers I'd ever met, almost to the point of being OCD. Now she's a little more normal about sweeping and cleaning out the crud wedged in snaps and clasps with a baby toothbrush, but only barely.

Lena's mom plays a doctor on *Riverview*, one of the few African American women leads on the show. I admit I was curious, so I had to check it out. I could barely make it through the episode. It was even worse than listening to Molly try to describe it—doctors in white coats with so much blush and contour the lights were practically hollowing out their cheeks. There was also lots of dialogue like, "You think you can cross me, Gerald!" and "You're shameless."

Serena's last name St. Claire is a stage name. Lena's dad died of a nasty form of cancer, and Serena hosts charity events for research and does commercials about getting checked for it.

Lena's mom looks just like her daughter on camera, only older, but with the same dark skin, short natural hair, and a lanky, aristocratic bearing. Well, if her daughter was wearing about a million coats of mascara and photographed through gauze while wearing a white coat, I guess.

I admit Serena St. Claire is a much better actress than most of the people on the soap. She has lots of dramatic exits and entrances involving walking onto elevators after reading the riot act to the newest hot young doctor flavor-of-the-month. "Did you even think to do a pregnancy test on her, Chad? No, you never think!"

Lena and I pull into the main parking lot of the horse park at seven in the morning. It's so cool and cloudy you could dream the summer air would never sneak up on you, grow thick and choke you, that the sun would never make my skin burn and peel. Lena mounts up confidently from the ground. She seems unfazed when Owen trots away, his pink nose in the air and his grey tail flapping like a flag behind him, as if daring his field mate Morrissey to chase him. All is going well.

I keep a close eye on her. Lena's riding like I always saw her riding at Vince's barn, with only a little extra stiffness in her arms and seat. But being hesitant on a new-to-her mount isn't abnormal. She's effortless, graceful, with the light seat and hands that come from riding super-sensitive horses like Pilot and the greener, ranker horses Vince used to leg her up on.

Together, we warm up on the flat, then go over some small logs, trot through the dirt paths, and play with the water complex. It's a fairly simple pond, flanked by small brush jumps to pop in and out.

"I thought you said you hadn't been on a horse since you got broken."

"I haven't."

"It doesn't show."

Lena seems relieved. The fizzy adrenaline of riding and being outdoors is making her nerves dissipate, much like the early coolness and morning clouds are fading.

There is a kind of pure pleasure in riding a horse that knows his job and is jumping just a shade beneath the top of his scope and ability. The water complex isn't so easy that Owen gets bored, but it's easy enough he doesn't hesitate in the slightest. Soon, he's happily spattered with mud on his belly and his legs are a slimy shade of green, matching his saddle pad.

"You need to sit back over fences," I say, observing Lena. "Don't be such a ring rider. Better to get left behind than topple over a horse's shoulder when you're on uneven terrain. Use your seat."

"I understand about using my seat. I actually started off as a dressage rider. But the horses I've been riding since were so reactive, I guess I've gotten nervous about planting my butt down."

"I didn't know that about the dressage!"

"In Germany. Mom was filming a miniseries there for six months, and I got hooked. Everyone starts in a dressage saddle. My legs were so short, they gave me two whips to reach below the saddle. But I got my growth spurt pretty quickly!"

"*Sprechen de deutch*? I was a working student over there for about five minutes."

"Nope, I was just a kid. I was too focused on the horses to learn about anything else. I wish I'd learned to speak German, it would have helped me out at one point. You?"

"Hell no, I can barely speak English right. If you know dressage, you should definitely event before you go to college. Are you going away this fall?"

"I have to take a year off, because the application deadlines have already passed. I'll work for a year and travel. Mom says that if I'm going to college the following year, she'll let me stay in her apartment, but if I go back to horses, then I'm on my own. That's our deal."

Before Vince, I know Lena trained with this guy, Mackenzie, who later got written up for SafeSport violations. He's married now—to one of his former students, a girl he met when she was fifteen. I've never asked Lena about him. Still, I'd guessed getting tossed by Pilot into a bunch of poles wasn't the first time she'd had some tough breaks in the horse world.

Lena is one of a handful of excellent Black riders on the A-circuit. Some people might say they have to put up with so much—in addition to the expected indignities all riders have to suffer through in the sport—even some of the most gifted don't stick with it.

"Does your mom ride?" I ask her, as we trot together away from the water, almost in synch, covering ground quickly on the winding dirt path.

Before Lena can answer, Owen surges ahead. This is what Eric meant. Owen can get strong without jumps to slow him down and keep his horsey brain busy. He's not a difficult ride, but he's not a "set it and forget it" ride, either. Back in a less politically correct time, he'd be called a man's horse. Not in the sense of a lazy old husband horse, but the type of horse that requires a man's height, weight, and muscle to get him to use himself back to front and pay attention to his rider.

Owen likes to root down and demands a constant stream of information from the rider—direction rather than finesse. It's true I've usually had men riding him, whether myself or my former boyfriend and business partner, Phillip Stone. When my mom tried him, she wasn't at all fond of him, and Molly's ridden him more out of a sense of duty than him being a good match for her. Still, Owen is safe, safe, safe, experienced, and not spooky. That's the most important thing when someone isn't used to riding cross-country.

Lena is having trouble whoa-ing him, but she at least has steering under control. She catches her breath enough to answer my question. "Mama says there's no need to do a dirty, expensive sport when I could, I don't know, just work out at the gym. She wears lipstick and mascara when she's on the treadmill, learning her lines at four in the morning. But she's happy I've decided to go to college. Not ride. Not act. I know what she does seems glamorous, but *Riverview General* has a brutal schedule. She's been Dr. Dawn Willis for twenty years running. She says daytime soaps are kind of dying, too, so she's always worried about them canceling the show."

I can't imagine being the same fake person for twenty years. I find it hard to be a fake person for twenty minutes, making nice with rich horse owners at a party or smiling at a photoshoot for some apparel company that's sponsoring me with free schwag.

"My boyfriend Eric teaches drama." Though Eric is not a particularly dramatic person, at least in comparison with the horse people in my life. In fact, when I visit him at the school he teaches at, it's almost relaxing. The biggest crisis is if someone forgets a line or a prop. Even when the theater kids yell at each other, it's not with the same urgency as when we say *horse coming through* at the barn.

"I know all about Eric!"

"What's that's supposed to mean?"

"I mean, it was a surprise you broke up with Phillip, that's all. You two had been together forever." Lena realizes she's made a mistake and is backpedaling quickly.

"Not forever." I should feel flattered people care enough to gossip about my love life, but I don't. Straight people rarely do so kindly.

My relationship with Phillip was always, well, complicated. Phillip's in a sort of weird place, financially and work-wise. If he wants to do horses and live the sort of equestrian life I've accustomed him to, he needs to work. But I've gotten a sense, following the dots of his life since he broke up with me, that doing Mickey Mouse office jobs (like "social media" and "marketing"), not riding, and not living in equestrian style (just normal person style), has been getting more and more acceptable. His mom's currently living with some rich guy. Phillip speaks several languages. I often seen him riding with his rich, foreign friends, borrowing their horses. Wearing their borrowed, ill-fitting (on him) riding gear, as if he needs to signal he's sleeping with them after he gets off their horses.

Phillip's pleasant, has an easy way about him. People enjoy buying him things and listening to him compliment them. Having Phillip around, if he's not riding for you, is like having a pretty set of dishes or a sports car in the garage. He's not really useful. But he's pretty, fancy, and fun, versus paper plates for takeout and a Subaru, which is often what I feel like, as a human being.

It's all a waste, because Phillip was a talented rider. I wasted horses, training, and money on him. He was better than me in some ways. More sensitive, more willing to let things happen than trying to control the horse all the time. But he never really wanted *it*. The equestrian life. To win. He didn't mind winning, sure. But he didn't want *it*, not enough. Nor did he want me, in the end.

At least Lena didn't gawk or giggle about my past relationships, like some women do. Although, truthfully, from what I've heard about Hollywood gossip from my barn manager, fellow riders, and students, I still think the horse world has showbiz beat on scandal. Horses make it more difficult for people to keep the crazy inside of them.

There's something about a late, giddy night after a show or a horse trial when you didn't fall off that can do something to your already piss-poor judgement. For who with good judgement would choose horses over an office job? Lena is sensible. She's thinking about college after a stint with a rank horse ended with a hard fall that could have hurt her much worse than it did. Even her mother, a soap star, is firing up the pressure cooker of guilt, so her daughter will get the hell out of horses.

I'm reflecting upon all this, watching Lena edge ahead of me as I balance and collect Morrissey. I'm calm. In the zone.

When I see the guy with the sword, I don't quite register his alien presence at first.

Suddenly, we're surrounded by men holding shiny swords. They're all wearing capes billowing in the wind. Four Medieval Times-style guys are standing in the burning

Maryland summer heat wearing capes, cassocks, and fake furs. Staring dumbstruck, like Lena and I are the crazies.

A second ago, Lena and I were enjoying the sunshine in our stretchy breeches, approved safety helmets, and ergonomically designed jumping saddles. Now, we're on a friggin' Crusade.

I freak out for a full .05 seconds, and I never freak out. It's hard to tell what will spook a horse, sometimes. Morrissey can take exception to some shrewishly cold, blowing wind on his flanks, but other times, some primal memory from the commotion at the track will kick in, and he'll barely seem to flick an ear at a screaming kid with a rustling bag of popcorn standing near an in-gate.

Then I look over at Lena and Owen. Or rather, where Lena and Owen used to be. I spy a white and slate grey tail heading to a nearby a bramble hedge.

Lena is hanging off the grey's left shoulder, her right stirrup swinging feral by the horse's side. She's grabbing mane, and I'm sure she's going to fall off. Then she rights herself, sits back. Owen goes around, rather than over the hedge, and I follow them.

"I'm not supposed to be riding yet! My doctor's going to kill me if I get hurt!" she blurts out, finally hauling Owen to a halt.

"Are you okay?" I ask.

"I'm okay," she says firmly. She slackens her reins slightly.

A lady wearing a green gown jumps out of the hedge. She's brandishing a stick with a crystal on it. The orb is winking and glittering like a wild thing. The lady raises her arms aloft, like she's doing her best Gandalf or "Y" of YMCA-fame impersonation.

I don't know what crystals do, but if there was a stone especially designed to cure the bubonic plague and spook horses, this must be it.

Lena is in the worst of all possible situations. Her muscles slackened with relief in the instant she believed herself safe. From her time off, her riding muscles and reflexes have atrophied slightly. Owen turns and heads away from the medieval lady and her glittery staff. Lena's trying to get a better grip on her reins. I gallop apace after my fiery steed.

Owen's gunning for the nearby dirt parking lot. I'm simultaneously trying to stay calm while preparing for the worst, while I hope there's no cars parked there.

No such luck. In fact, the usually empty side lot is now a goddamned vendor area full of shiny silver trucks selling hot dogs, burgers, stuffed potatoes, swords, and capes. Like fucking fleas or locusts, there's even more of the weird people in armor and gowns. Some of them are play-fighting, roaring and shouting.

Owen goes up.

Lena, bless her cotton tall boot socks and breeches, stays on, arms around his neck.

Then this guy in gold armor reaches for the bridle of the rearing horse, yanking at the leather. Like he knows what he's doing.

The next thing I know, Owen deposits Lena onto the counter of one of the food trucks with a resounding bang.

There is an aching moment of silence as Lena just lies there. Bags of chips and pretzels waft to the ground like dried leaves. Mustard, ketchup, and relish from the waiting order has smeared all over her breeches. She remains frozen in place, utterly still and silent as a statue. A condiment-encrusted statue.

Slowly, she slides off the counter, face impassive and expressionless.

I can only hope she hit the metal with the hip without the cracked femoral neck.

She limps over to Owen, who has that horsey *I just done a real bad thing* look on his face. Lena leads him over to a table with a vendor selling silver medallions and rings, uses it for a mounting block, and quietly exits at a walk on the now-very calm horse.

Lena doesn't speak a word until we're riding back in my trailer, settled in the front compartment. "I'm sorry I got mustard and relish on your saddle," she says.

"Take a warm shower and decompress. Let me know how you are before you go to bed."

"I think there may still be some ketchup on it. I'm pretty sure it's not blood."

"You're sure you're okay?"

"Maybe a few tears. I know salt water isn't good for nice leather. I tried to wipe off as much as I could. I'm fine."

"I swear, he's usually chill. I guess those people in costume just pushed some hidden buttons. Advil and a hot bath."

"How often do those medieval people come to the horse park?"

"I've never seen them before."

She nods to say she thinks I'm full of shit.

I unload Owen who seems to have undergone a transformation in the trailer, like I've baked a fucking cake, putting into the tiny oven a loon I didn't recognize, and getting out the sweaty, steaming, but contrite horse I do. I hose him off, sweat-scrape him, and turn him out in his field. He's done for the day, work-wise. He's placid among the green, only pausing to roll and grind some grass into his freshly-washed dapples.

I used to trust him completely. Now I can't, not entirely. Just like I used to trust Phillip, until the day he left me. Still, I love the sight of the healthy, athletic horse trotting 'round his paddock, even the smell of him on me, as the temperature climbs higher and higher, making me sweat, making me smell of horse even more than before.

Phillip always used to forget and leave the grain bins open, practically begging mice to enjoy the buffet. I notice with satisfaction the bins are closed. Molly's on top of things. No shadows of my ex linger in my barn or brain, I tell myself, except as tricks of my weak mind. During the day, I hardly think of Phillip at all. It's at night, when I'm alone, my imagination gets too active.

I give the closed bins a little pat with my hand. It satisfies me, like the sight of a properly closed barn door.

Fortunately, I'm not alone tonight. I meet my boyfriend Eric back at my place for dinner. Neither of us likes to meal-plan, which is a relief (thanks to some of my ex-boyfriends' peculiar insistence on 'real food' I've had to go hungry for many hours waiting for them to cook in the past). We're just having subs, chips, and soda on this hot day. Speaking of which, of all the frigging days in the world to be wearing cassocks, bearskins, and armor, you're going to do it when it's ninety degrees out? I know it's rude, but before Eric can get a word in about his day, I'm monopolizing the conversation, "You're never going to believe what just happened to me."

"I thought nothing entertaining was going to happen. That you knew Owen so well," he says, dryly, rubbing in his victory like coarse salt on freshly wounded flesh.

I'm too angry to make myself and my bad idea look any less bad than it was. I'm so worked up, I don't even open up the waxed paper around my sub until I finish the story. At first, Eric sits, thoughtfully crunching on a salt and vinegar chip, before he takes a big bite of his salami and provolone sandwich oozing with tomato, oil, and shredded lettuce. But when I get to the hot dog truck, he puts his sub down. At the end of it all, he begins to laugh. And laugh. Coughing on a shard of Italian bread caught in his throat briefly shuts him up, as he washes it down with Sprite.

"Eric, you of all people, you who are scared to even ride a goddam horse, it's not funny!"

"I know it's not really funny. But you were going on and on about how safe this horse is."

"What kind of asshole do you take me for? The poor woman was getting over a nasty fall."

"LARP-ing."

"What language are you speaking?"

"Live Action Role Playing. The people you saw were LARP-ers. I've done it myself."

"You? You? I've shared a bed with a man who runs around the woods in a Halloween costume?"

"I teach history and drama and direct plays. You know I used to act professionally."

"On the stage. Like a somewhat-normal person."

"Admittedly, I've only dabbled in LARP-ing."

He's making it sound like drugs. I almost wish it was.

Eric's reminiscing, fondly. "You are given a scenario. Often there's a battle between good and evil forces. Or a quest. Then, you make up your character."

"Like an elf?"

"Not just elves! Like, shape-shifters and warlocks and such. No, no. Not just elves."

"Oh, well, in that case. As long as there are no elves."

"Then you act it all out. Extemporize and such. In costume."

"Dress up? With leather vests and funny ears and glasses? In public?"

"I thought you played Dungeons & Dragons in high school. You love Star Wars and fantasy and all that stuff."

"Eric, sitting in some kid's dark basement rolling dice and watching one of the most popular movie franchises, is a completely different animal than pretending to be King Arthur and his Merry Men of Middle Earth, spooking horses into hot dog trucks."

"Versus jumping wooden ducks in the middle of a lake like you do eventing? Which is totally useful and normal behavior?"

"These people were playing at being knights and don't even know how to behave around a horse. That's inexcusable. Lena is picking relish out of her ass right now. Because of them."

"Simon, don't you think sometimes you're a little too eager to have people ride Owen?"

"He's for sale, of course I am."

"But you put your mom on him. And Lena. They didn't want to buy him or even particularly want to ride him. Didn't you buy him for your ex Phillip, who was a top-level eventer?"

"Don't try to psychologize me, Eric. I assign horses based on the rider, nothing else. Phillip wasn't a top-level eventer when I bought Owen for him. He was a showjumper, just like Lena." I shut my mouth. Somehow, I feel I'm digging myself a bigger and bigger hole with every other word.

"I was actually going to ask if you wanted to go to a Renaissance Faire with me. You said I could choose our next outing, since we went to a horse show together last time."

30

"Horse trial, that's what we call it in eventing. Not show."

"Trial-by-Ordeal is a more appropriate term, I agree. Showbiz is fun."

I keep chewing, ignoring the pain in my jaw.

"I guess that's a Ye Olde No on the Faire," says Eric. "Since you're emotionally scarred by the LARP."

I call Lena since I don't want to have an argument with my boyfriend.

"I'm okay. Really. Only my pride is sore."

"Look, I know they say 'never say never' with horses. But I've never seen that happen! Cosplayers invading the horse park!"

"It wasn't your fault."

"I shouldn't have oversold how broke Owen was."

"I shouldn't have oversold how recovered I was. I'm still pretty shook from the fall. Not the one today, but the spill I took with Pilot."

"You know, I'm taking the boys to a little informal showjumping competition, just to keep them sharp."

"The boys?"

"Owen and Morrissey."

"So?"

"*You* could ride Owen. Just sayin'."

"No."

"It's not eventing or cross-country. Showjumping! Pure showjumping! In a ring. Which you like. Your specialty."

"No. I need my brain to write my college essays and study for the SATs. I can't have it rung against any more concession stands."

"The footing is sandy and soft as a cloud, if you fall off," I say, only half-joking.

"I'm an old lady with a femoral neck stress fracture healing in my busted hip and can't stay up too late, anyway."

Lena is probably nineteen, maybe twenty, for the record. She's hardly out of high school, although like most kids on the A-circuit, I know she did online school for her senior year.

"It's a casual thing at Barbara Harper's. They set up a course, and then just raise the height for each division. Not very technical. Just so you don't leave things on a sour note with Owen."

"What if I hurt him?"

"It will not be like it was with Pilot, Lena! We can't live in the past."

This is as close as I come to admitting the whole truth. I feel that if Lena gets Owen around a course, I'll somehow have washed the whole incident with the medieval re-enactors away, cleaned my dirty conscience, and can sell him without Phillip haunting my mind. Prove to Eric and myself this has nothing to do with vanquishing the ghost of my ex in horse form. It's got nothing to do with showing the world that Phillip wasn't the only rider who could ride Owen well.

"No."

"I don't want you to be afraid of riding. Even if you go to college and give up your dream of being a professional horsewoman."

"No means no."

"The sight of the sunset is beautiful from Barb's ring."

"Simon, since when did you notice sunsets?"

"I've always enjoyed a colorful sunset."

"No, no, no. From now on, I'm sticking to dead broke horses. Barn name Slowpoke."

"Where should I pick you up?"

Chapter 2
Rabbit Rabbit

Lena comes to my barn and rides Owen twice in my ring. He's the same steady Owen I've known for years. I'm proud of him. I think she likes him, and she's learning to manage his tendency to root heavy into her hand. She stays and helps Molly and me at the barn afterward. I tell her she doesn't have to; she says she feels obligated, though it was I who needled her into riding my horse.

Every time, before she rides Owen, I go into his stall and whisper, gently rapping my knuckles against his skull, "Keep in the crazy. You be a good boy."

Maybe I'm the crazy person. Whenever I see Owen ridden by another person—even a willowy, feminine woman like Lena—I glimpse Phillip's ghost. The ghost who ghosted me. I remind myself it was I who broke up with him. He came begging me to take him back. I said no, I set the boundaries.

I'm sure he's not haunted in the same way. Some people aren't hardwired to have regrets.

I know deep down what Eric says about Owen is true. I can't forget and forgive what a fine rider Phillip was, and how he was able to coax such deft performances from my difficult horses. Then Phillip gave up what matters most to me in the world—*horses*—just like he gave up on me, like I meant nothing at all. If horses are so easy to let go of, so meaningless, what does that say about me?

Lately, I've also been missing Eric, who stubbornly insists on keeping distance between the two of us, until he's gotten on his feet financially and emotionally after the breakup of his starter marriage. Sometimes he'll sleep over, sometimes he won't.

On one of her riding days, confirming my suspicion that under her cool, professional exterior Lena is a total badass, she rides over to the barn on a Vespa, a little motorized scooter. She's got a special helmet and a thin scarf around her neck to protect herself against the wind and everything.

I take temporary possession of the Vespa, tootling around, saying I'm desensitizing the horses. It's pale pink, and she bought it to travel more easily around the showgrounds at Wellington. I'm secure enough in my masculinity to want to marry it.

"Mama actually said a prayer when she first saw it. If I die on this thing, she'll dig me up from my grave and kill me again."

I rev the engine. "I can tell it's blessed. Holy. Like going to church. If you ever need to retire it out to pasture, call me. I have room."

"At least Mr. Particular doesn't seem to be bothered by it," she says, giving Owen a pat. I guess it sounded enough like a tractor or a weed whacker, which he hears all the time at the farm. He barely batted an ear at its kitten-like roar.

Lena's actions and attitude aren't those of someone who is fearful by nature. She walks Owen cool around the surrounding track of the farm on a long rein. I pass Molly off to her when Molly talks wedding plans. The wedding is a year and a half in the future, and given Molly will then want to find a job that doesn't require her to live on-property, I've filed locating a new barn manager into the ever-expanding folder of Non-Urgent Problems I Still Need to Worry About Soon.

I can grudgingly understand why Molly wants to get married, even though it doesn't jive with my barn's needs. It's Lena I can't figure out. I have a feeling there's another reason for her deciding to quit riding as a pro beyond the injury, but I won't press her. I just try to get her hyped up about riding Owen.

Lena and I trailer over with Morrissey and Owen to Barbara Harper's farm. I've been going to Barb's showjumping at dusk series for two summers running now. Basically, Barb sets up a course in her big arena when things cool down. Arena lights illuminate the entire ring, although there's always one or two shadowy jumps that will flummox a green horse or nappy pony.

Heights start at around two feet—little jumps—and then every class she sets them higher and higher, depending on who has come. Once, Morrissey and I won our division. It's casual fun, but for me, even casual fun is sweeter if it's accompanied by competition and prizes, no matter how inconsequential those prizes may be.

Owen, under Lena's stewardship, I'm pretty sure, can put in a credible showing. As she tacks him up by the trailer, though, I hear a familiar voice.

"You!" I cry. A bobbing, talking head has come into my line of vision. A head that I'm used to being bright red or blue, but now is blonde with chunky streaks of deep, mermaid-green.

"Why, hello, Simon O' Shaughnessy, how are you doing?" Ah, Ainsley Ashcroft. Former hunter princess and my forever nemesis.

"Is Sandra here?" I ask, referring to her eventing boss, Sandra Black.

"Nope. I've left that operation for good. I was only a fair-weather eventing groom. The plan was always to go back to riding the hunters."

"I should have known by the old skool hunter rust breeches and the hunter green streaks in your hair."

"Yup, finally returning to my roots. No more ugly bulb dressage braids for these delicate little fingers." She waves a chipped but still sparkling green manicure in my face, though her nails are a short, practical length. "I'm working for Fletcher Cox."

"Fletch Cox?" I ask. "He's decent."

"Nice to know you approve, Simon. I was losing sleep, like it was eating away at me, to think you might frown upon my decision. I'm here with only one student; the breeches are just in case I need to get on her pony, if he puts on any shenanigans in the warmup ring. One of my barn's few pony jumpers. The pony's very green—like my new hair, ha, see how I slipped that in—which is why we're here, to get him some experience before a show that counts."

Fletch runs a mid-level show barn of pony riders, juniors riding in the equitation and hunter divisions, and a handful of hunter and jumper amateur adults. He's got money, so it's more of a vanity business for him than something he's running balls to the wall for cash. I'm surprised someone so low-key would tolerate Ainsley's intensity, but I admit she's an effective rider in the hunters and can groom horses so that they catch a judge's eye.

Ainsley was grooming at and managing the barn of an eventer named Sandra Black for a bit, but I guess she jumped ship back to the world she prefers. Ainsley excels at a type of riding—show hunters—where fashion, flash, and expensive horses take center stage, rather than speed and athleticism. I saw her ride when she was younger in the jumpers, which are purely judged on speed rather than style, and she just wasn't very good. Ainsley has *feel* for the horse's way of going, but can't bring herself to go for an ugly distance to make the time.

While I don't entirely respect her as a human being, I have to respect Ainsley as a rider in her specialty. Because

Ainsley wants *it*. She doesn't come from money, never went to college, has no other skills that don't involve horses. She has even less ability to walk away from it than I do. I, at least, have some money in the bank, and a brain with some business sense from managing my farm, plus some natural facility at math planted in my head, through no real effort on my part.

Ainsley has charm, a soft release, and the ability to braid a horse so his neck looks like it's adorned with the shining jewels of a crown. Desperation has led her to work for some shady characters and get taken advantage of, but she'll never wrap a polo wrong or walk past a stall and leave it unpicked.

"Lena, what are you doing with Simon? I heard about your fall! Oh my God, it sounded so bad!" Ainsley knows Lena from way back, from when they were both riding the A-circuit. And she's turned up at just the right-wrong time to remind Lena of that fall off of Pilot, before Lena's about to ride a horse who reared up on her.

"I'm here, riding for fun with a friend, to get my nerve back," says Lena, which is a really nice way of saying I bullied her into coming, slightly, and that everyone on the East Coast has heard about her tumble off Pilot or saw it on the livestream.

"I didn't know Simon had friends," says Ainsley. She shifts her focus back to me. "Have you talked to Phillip recently?"

She can't keep the eagerness out of her voice. I bristle inside. I'm holding Owen's lead rope in one hand, and Morrisey in the other. Letting anger stiffen my grip would be an exceedingly bad idea. I hand Owen over to Lena before clenching a now-free fist.

"I think Phillip is still mooching off his mom? I haven't talked to him recently." After all, he's my ex.

"We spoke last night. He's doing the social media for some ballet company. Dating a dancer."

I wish Ainsley hadn't added that little tidbit of gossip. She used to date Phillip when he was a teenager, sort of, and while I don't place their relationship quite on the same level as mine—Phillip and I lived together, were business partners—the fact remains she's still on regular speaking terms with him, and I am not. I must accept Phillip is now Ainsley's friend, more than he is mine. Phillip and I said we'd remain friends, but that never really happens. We're more like comfortably distant enemies.

Phillip seems to get most of his jobs through his mother's or a lover's connections. I am, of course, in the latter category. As practiced a rider as he was, if he wasn't sleeping with me, his then-thin resume wouldn't have gotten him a job at O' Shaughnessy Eventing. He used to ride for me, and now he's shacked up with his mother in Manhattan. While living with your parents when you're in your twenties sounds kind of tragic, Phillip's not holed up in his childhood bedroom in suburban Maryland like Eric.

"Why you'd leave Sandra's, Ainsley?" I ask, switching topics. I thought Ainsley enjoyed working for Sandra Black, even though she wasn't riding. "Didn't want to follow her to England?"

"Sandra's not riding in England. She's hiding out there from her husband's lawyers and the IRS," says Ainsley. She takes a lollypop and sticks it in her cheek. Not exactly Pony Club-certified safe around horses. Ainsley runs the bright sour green apple-flavored ball across her tongue, suggestively. I always wonder if Ainsley coordinates her entire ensemble with her current hair color, right down to her props, before she goes out in the world. Or if she ever tires of flirting with gay men.

"Didn't you hear her husband was embezzling from his company? There's also some tax stuff. It's a mess. A big fat mess. They've lost the farm. It's going to be a messy, messy divorce." Ainsley dramatically gestures with her lollypop, kind of like how people do with cigarettes in old movies. "I left before things completely fell apart," she says, popping the green candy back between her pursed lips. That's Ainsley, for sure. She can smell trouble before it happens, so she can run in the opposite direction.

"Ainsley, I'm going to be on deck soon," says a kid. The girl's wild, unraveling braid is hanging down the back of her coat. She's leading a white pony with a similarly feral expression in his dark eyes.

"You better put your hair up, Gretchen, if you're supposed to be in the warmup area by now," says Ainsley. She crunches at whatever is in the center of the pop.

"I'm not going to. It makes my head hurt."

"Leave it down. It's safer," I say.

"Safer. An eventer saying something's safer," says Ainsley. "Simon O' Shaughnessy, of all people, with his crazy Thoroughbreds." The girl mounts the pony lightly with a leg up from Ainsley.

"Not fair, Ainsley, this horse Owen appears to be a warmblood, and is still certifiably crazy," says Lena.

Ainsley cackles. "Owen's one of Simon's saner horses," says Lena.

"Simon keeps telling me so, and Owen keeps not believing him. So, I keep not believing Simon."

"Your helmet should fit your head, not some hunter-fashion hairdo." I'm ignoring all this shade being cast at my grey horse, my Owen. "Why do you, of all people, care about a kid's hair being up in her helmet, Ainsley?"

"It's because I dye my hair these crazy colors that I know you've gotta have hair over the ears and wear a hair

net that tones down the color to look respectable. Liv Sexton would have cut off my ears sooner than let me go in the ring without my hair up, even in the jumpers. But what can I do? It's the younger generation." She leaves with her pony kid.

Liv Sexton was the old lady Ainsley used to ride for, before Liv had the audacity to die and deprive Ainsley of access to her expensive horses.

"The hair over the ears thing never worked for me either," says Lena.

Suddenly, even though I wasn't going on about the need for a silky-smooth bun tucked up in your helmet to be a proper rider, I feel embarrassed. Lena's natural hair is sculpted to her head. Her swanlike neck and profile are given additional, understated elegance with small rose-gold earrings sparkling with little pink gemstones. I've never seen her look anything but perfectly put together. Her schooling boots and gloves are spotless, carefully buffed and polished for this casual show. Her earrings match her long-sleeved show shirt. She's one of the few women I've ever seen who looks sophisticated in pink, rather than childish.

I realize she's probably put a great deal of work into her appearance, regardless of whether she really wants to be here or not. Every day I've ever seen her showing her face at a barn, she's always looked the same—matched, pressed, yet not so fussily dressed she's not ready to work. Ainsley—and even me, with my fondness for wine-colored Doc Martens and band t-shirts—can choose how much we stand out or blend in, in a way that Lena cannot. Ainsley can stuff her dyed hair under a helmet; I can hide my tats under a shirt, all in the name of making an owner or sponsor more comfortable.

"I'm sorry," I say.

"Oh, Ainsley is just a ridiculous person," Lena says, shrugging.

"Aren't you friends with her?"

"It's hard not to be. She won't let you be otherwise. She is what she is. Didn't she groom for you?"

"Ainsley has a way of making herself indispensable, for a time, then leaving." That's the fairest summary I can make of Ainsley's career and our friendship. She is a ridiculous person, but she is a hard worker and not a ridiculous rider, trainer, and groom, so I must tolerate her.

Lena and I graze the horses near the warmup ring. There will be a wait; there's more people in the lower-level divisions than I thought there would be.

Ainsley's kid Gretchen is zipping over the warmup jumps with no respect, gunning the pony like my brother Sean used to ride his car over the speedbumps of my high school's driveway every morning. "Slow down," I hear Ainsley bark. "Slow. Down." How does such a loud voice emerge from such a little person as Ainsley? She's speaking more slowly than usual, as if that will better penetrate the pony kid's brain.

Ainsley's and Lena's fashionable zipped sunshirts in technical fabrics are a stark contrast with my threadbare black cotton t-shirt. These women are investing so much effort into their appearance for a casual horse show. Then I slap my neck, letting bloody mosquito guts trail down my hand, squashing my contempt along with the bug. I'm the fool, and there's a practical reason they're dressed as they are and sunshirts are popular. I thought my cotton Killers t-shirt was so worn, it would feel like a second skin, but now I'm stewing in my own sweat and it offers no protection against all the evil little things swarming in the air this summer night.

When it's Gretchen's turn in the two-foot division, her little pony Rabbit Rabbit is game to go. She shortens him before the first jump, and he leaps the red-and-white pole more like an agile hare than an Easter Bunny. Motorcycling him to the next fence, Gretchen takes the long option over the next bright yellow vertical. I didn't think the small pony could make such a close-your-eyes-and-pray distance, but the pair springs over, turning straight for the oxer at the side of the ring.

Despite the fact we've had rain recently, the pony's little hooves are kicking up a Tasmanian Devil-sized cloud of dust. Morrissey and I actually get a handful of sand rained down on us as she passes. Morrissey jerks his head up, looks around, nostrils flaring. I do nothing, but simply watch and wait. Then he seems to deflate, shrinks back to his usual size, and resumes eating grass. I feel proud of this relaxation, proud in a different way than I am of his recent competitive performances. There was a time when he wouldn't settle so quickly and easily.

Owen is his usual self, grazing on a bank, and calm, which is a good thing, because Lena's staring at Gretchen and Rabbit Rabbit, and has relaxed her attention upon the horse she's about to ride.

"That was something," I say, as Gretchen slides down and loosens her girth. She was three seconds under the other riders in the division, which is practically like lapping someone running on a track.

"That was not how I told her to ride it," mutters Ainsley.

"I didn't think so," I say.

"I took you here to work on your skills," says Ainsley to Gretchen. "Once the jumps go up a few inches, yeehaw-ing my pony won't cut it."

I know Ainsley doesn't really own any horse or pony. She always calls any horse under her training *my*, though, a habit which has always annoyed me.

"But you were great fun to watch scooting around," I counter. *Closer to the ground, closer to hell,* I've always said about ponies, but I still love the pony jumpers' turn-and-burn style. Their riders make Hail Mary-bad decisions about distances that their mounts' catty little pony legs and bodies somehow make work.

Gretchen is one of those kids who doesn't smile or react to an adult's praise or criticism. Braid bobbing, stone-faced except for her pink cheeks, she walks back to the trailer with Ainsley.

"Don't encourage her. Can you believe they advertised this pony as a quiet children's hunter? We're making do in the jumpers, but Rabbit Rabbit is *not* what the Malloys paid Fletch to find." Ainsley stalks off.

"Let that be a lesson to you, Lena," I say, lightening the mood. "Trust no one in the horse business. Especially when he says a horse is broke."

"I learned that long ago. Just happened to forget it when you offered to let me ride Owen. I was never on ponies that long, I was this height at twelve," says Lena, gesturing from the top of her head to her boots.

"That's sad, because there's no one that will teach you like a pony that when it's horse versus human, horse always wins." Gretchen strikes me as a kid who won't slow down until she ends up in the dust, riding a horse that won't tolerate her demand to turn on a dime at warp speed. She certainly won't if what she's doing right now is winning. In the jumpers, all you need is to beat the clock. But you also need to stick on the horse until the end of the round.

I give Lena a leg up, then saddle up Morrissey, using a splintery fence as a mounting block. We flat outside of the ring at a walk, trot, and canter, while waiting for the warmup ring to open up for the final division of the night. The height is lower than what Morrissey has been jumping for eventing, and while I brought him to Barb's with the mindset of just keeping him eventing sharp, my inner showjumping fire is unexpectedly brewing. I turn down the flame just enough to remind myself I'm really here for Lena, to get her confidence back with Owen.

Owen and Lena have a harmony together today they didn't have outside in the larger, wider expanse of the horse park, over rougher terrain. Lena is clearly in her element. She has the horse on the bit and he responds to her aids as she transitions from trot to canter to extended canter to walk to halt.

Then I see the sword in the distance, raised just over Lena's shoulder.

In the nearby lot, there's a group of people in capes, brandishing medieval hardware.

"You look worried about something," says Lena, as she passes me. Her little earrings are winking pink beneath her helmet in the artificial light and natural moonglow.

"What is there to be worried about?" Now why do I have to be such a terrible liar? I should be better at it. I'm in horses, after all.

She pulls up Owen and gives me *that look*.

"It's my teeth," I say. Which is honest, because my back molars—I think it's my wisdom teeth, crowding against them—have been hurting on and off for weeks. The Cap'n Crunch turned out to be yet another bad life decision, in retrospect. I've been waiting for my teeth to give up their ghosts of pain, as teeth usually do, but they haven't yet. Even I can't ignore the unpleasant throbbing tonight. It's radiating into my jaw and shoulders. While I don't ride with my teeth, shoulders are rather important for steering.

I figure the medieval folk are far enough away they won't bother us. But why are they everywhere? Technically, they aren't trespassing on the farm. The property next to Barb's has been for sale for two years. The barn is boarded up; the fields have gone to seed. In winter, it's a haunted wasteland, but in summer, it's not unusual to see people picnicking in defiance of ticks and gnats, or kids speeding around on quads.

Lena doesn't need to worry about this, I tell myself. They're far enough away. Focus.

Gretchen skips by the warmup ring, brandishing her winning prize from her division, a five-pound chocolate Hershey's bar. Because of my damn teeth, I haven't been able to eat all day, I've been hammering down soda like nobody's business, and I'm hangry as hell.

Lena jumps the warmup oxer once, twice. I enter the ring on Morrissey and immediately break into a trot.

Lena's clenching her jaw—although not as tightly as I do mine, since I'm trying to be careful not to grind down against the pressure of the teeth pressing upward. My own teeth are fighting me more than my horse. Morrissey is on form today, softening at his poll. His mouth is softer than my own.

When I enter the arena, the first competitor in my division, I give Morrissey an inch with my reins, let him relax for a split second at the start of the buzzer. If only I can keep his opinions in synch with mine about striding and pace. With this horse, I can never impose my will entirely. I have to wait for him to figure things out, make him believe it's partly his decision to jump when I say to jump and whoa when I say to whoa.

For example, as we head over the first broad plank fence, I let him take the longer option, since I know that will put him in a more positive mindset. He listens to me when my leg nudges him over to slice the second to save time. He doesn't like the third jump, a skinny, and gives a little spook beforehand, so we drift in the air, but I don't overcorrect the wobble like I might have in the past, although I nearly clip the standard with my knee. The jump stays up.

Overall, it's a good, clean round, with no time faults. But this is a speed class, which means the fastest clean round wins. There's no jump-off. We were tidy, but not terribly quick, so there's still room to beat us.

Much as I hate to admit it, my eventer's mentality may be a factor. When I showjumped hell for leather as a kid, and later when I was riding jumpers for my friend Cheryl Whitechapel, speed was always on my mind. Imperceptibly, even to myself, my body would adjust to the demands of the class. In eventing, the primary goal of the stadium round is simply not to accumulate more penalties. I have grown more careful, or, lazier, as I think of myself in less forgiving moments.

Regardless, Morrissey leaving the poles up is a victory to celebrate. I dismount and loosen his girth. He shakes his head violently, nearly smacking me with his muzzle, then whips around with his teeth. I step out of the way and he connects his jaws with a fly upon his flank, but I know his threat was meant for me, for some offense I committed. Perhaps just for the indignity of being alive, human, and on his back.

I turn my attention back to the course. The rider after me, Franny Davis, runs a small boarding and training operation. She's on a big bay gelding. The pair pulls a rail, four faults. After Franny, there's someone I don't recognize on a chestnut mare. The horse prances around, nose almost straight in the air, straining against the rider's hand. The mare is an attractive, dainty horse with scope, despite her small size (barely 16h, I'd wager). But I can tell she's not the rider's usual type, and the horse isn't a fan of the rider's backward release. Every fence is a fight. Twelve faults.

Lena is on deck. "The medieval weirdos are practicing nearby! Why didn't you tell me?" I notice Owen is looking wild-eyed, his back is up, he's a coiled spring between Lena's

46

long, draping legs. I tell myself it's impossible for a horse to take specific exception to cosplayers. It's not logical spookiness, like how Morrissey used to hate to jump ditches. The fear of leaping over a gap in the ground is one thing. A fear of guys who get off fondling swords is another. Still, I don't feel the same unshakable confidence in Owen's good sense as I did when I was arguing with Eric at the kitchen table.

"My time is beatable," I say, as a kind of apology.

"Thanks for leaving the window open," she says through tight, vengeful lips.

"You know what they say? Horses only spook at two things—things that move and things that don't. If you avoid them both, you're golden."

"Thanks, Simon."

I'm holding my breath as Lena circles 'round to the first fence after the starting bell. She's mad at me, I can tell, but that doesn't affect the way she rides Owen. Despite any naughtiness she experienced in the warmup ring after Owen heard and saw the men with broadswords in the distance, she's calm, focused, and steady in her connection with her rein and leg pressure.

Owen gallops to the first fence, turns like that catty little rabbit of a pony, slices the second, leaves out a stride to the third, and Lena and he have a flawless round. She's a full second under my time. Once within the confines of the arena and the time pressure of the buzzer, horse and rider lock on to every obstacle, reading each one without a hesitation or bobble.

"It's not nice to do better than your trainer," I say.

Lena's lost her murderous look.

I hear a clink of swords as we walk our horses back to the trailer. Owen spooks and tranters away—half-trotting, half-cantering—with Lena barely hanging onto his bridle. She can't stop him but steers him into a fence. He halts, snorting and stupid, at the high post-and-rail he can't leap over with the weight of a determined, lanky woman dragging him back.

I decide to hightail out before Lena changes her mind about not killing me. Morrissey, for once, loads compliantly. Owen won't budge. The grey tries to dive off the into the darkness twice, then three times.

"I'm not sure what you're getting out of this," I say to him. "Your hay is in the net in there, your dinner is at home."

It's after dark. My back is beginning to spackle with rising welts from the mosquito bites and itch with drying sweat. My wisdom teeth are throbbing. I try never to lose my temper with horses and act out of rage, but I'm damn close to it. I hand Lena a lunge whip and finally, between the two of us, my supposedly practiced, self-loading, broke-to-death upper-level eventer crawls up the trailer next to his chestnut friend.

Barbara knocks on the passenger window as Lena and I get settled. I've already cranked up the air-conditioning to full blast, but I roll down the window. "Nice job! Here's your prize," she says, cheerfully, sticking a large glass mason jar full of orange and yellow candy into Lena's hands.

Barb's a motherly woman with haphazardly cut red hair. It looks like she chopped it off herself, staring at a barn mirror in between giving lessons. She doesn't ride much, just does the occasional hunter pace here and then, but she runs a decent operation and I thank her. Thank her over the banging in the back, that is. Because the commotion Owen raised unsettled Morrissey, setting off the other gelding into a frenzy of kicking. Now I feel like an idiot amateur, with horses that can't even behave their damn selves off-property.

"I guess he's missing his other dad," Barb says cheerfully.

"I'm sorry?"

"I haven't seen Phillip all summer!"

Of course. Barb doesn't follow the local eventing or horse show gossip. Her world is her farm, her horses, the shows she runs. She doesn't realize Phillip and I broke up. I don't have the words to explain right now. All I can hear are the horses he used to ride so beautifully begging to be set free of their tin can, slamming their hooves against the walls like Barb's words are slamming against my hard heart.

Lena is too busy eating to pay close attention to the conversation.

"Don't you know? I'm dating Lena right now."

"Even though I'm not his type," says Lena. Barb withdraws so I can finally roll up the window again, to keep the cool air in and her words about Phillip out.

We drive down the dirt driveway as fast as I dare, because I've been ready for this evening to end several hours ago. Lena sits beside me in the truck, cradling her jar of tiny Butterfingers and Reece's Peanut Butter Cups. The re-enactors have disappeared with the last traces of purple dusk. It's dark, a real, starlit country dark now, with only a half-thought of moon.

The air has grown so thick and humid it's stagnating within me, making every breath a drag, even with the air-conditioning in my car roaring. I speed faster than I should, wanting to get to the brightly lit highway, and to get some wind into the stale cavities of my lungs. I open the windows and blast the cold air simultaneously, desiring motion in any shape or form, wherever I can find it.

"I hate you," I shout over the whooshing near my left shoulder, as Lena crunches a Butterfinger.

"Why?"

"Butterfingers are my favorite candy."

"Want one? I'm not going to eat all of this."

"No, just the thought of chewing makes me sick."

Her final sharp crunch on the one in her mouth hurts my teeth vicariously. She holds onto the door as I make a sharp turn. "Slow down. You should really have someone look at your mouth. Teeth don't get better on their own."

"I can handle it," I say, gritting my teeth. *If I can steady a trailer on a country highway and get two nutty eventing horses home safely, I can tolerate pain.* "I got this."

"But you don't have to man up and 'get it.' See a dentist. See an oral surgeon. What, you don't have insurance?"

"I have insurance. I can't afford to take time off teaching and riding," I mutter.

"You're not riding Morrissey or Owen tomorrow because they were competing tonight. Won't tomorrow be a slow day for you?"

"Like I can get an appointment tomorrow."

"My uncle is the best oral surgeon in all of Baltimore County. I can hook you up with an appointment." She eats another mini-Butterfinger.

I always thought one advantage of being a gay man was not having a female partner who would say things like *I'm making you a dental appointment. I'm making you an appointment with my uncle, the best oral surgeon in Baltimore County.*

"You wouldn't let a horse go without getting his teeth floated," she points out.

Ah, Lena's flowery, feminine logic. "I'm fine," I say.

"There's no point in suffering unnecessary pain."

"So why am I doing this?" I counter, gesturing to the horses behind me.

What's with Lena pulling some oral surgeon uncle out of her skinny ass? She's eating candy for dinner.

Eating. I remember that. My spine is pressing against my bellybutton. I'm a tall, thin man with a fast metabolism. Avoiding eating is not one of my goals.

Chapter 3
Lips Like Sugar

Next morning, I'm sitting in the waiting room of the best oral surgeon in Baltimore County, staring at my phone. Eric texts me: *I'm glad you're getting yourself fixed.*

Fixed. Like a goddamned spaniel. Every person in my life is part of the same elaborate conspiracy to take my wisdom teeth out of my head. Do they all work for Big Tooth or something?

Lena's Uncle Russell reveals himself to be a tall, powerfully built man who wears silver-rimmed wire glasses. In context, this makes me think of the evil-looking metal retainers I saw on kids when I was much younger. Mom couldn't afford such fancy contraptions for Sean and me. I wouldn't have worn one, anyway. Hell, Mom had trouble making me brush my teeth at all.

Lena got me through the door by rattling a verbal lunge whip of warnings, like I did a real one at Owen's reluctant ass. Apparently, the good Dr. Roberts has a patient waiting list a mile long, as well as a stuffed appointment calendar. I am jumping the queue, because I am her friend. I should be grateful.

"What's the trouble?" he asks me.

I mutter something about my wisdom teeth. "Hard to believe, given no one's ever accused me of being wise." Making jokes is how I get through my usual dentist appointments, cleanings and fillings. I say funny things about my crappy teeth. My regular dentist reminds me I need to see an oral surgeon as soon as possible, and I cheerfully grin and ignore her.

Another part of the game I play with my dentist is dodging her calls and reminders to make an appointment until it's been seven, eight, nine months. My relationship with dentists is much like horses who play hard-to-catch with kids in pastures. I know the dentists will wear me down eventually and I'll crack (or one of my fillings will) and I'll come in, but it makes me feel better putting up a fight. My regular dentist has always accepted my idiocy because she knows I often contemplate throwing her off completely, never to return.

Dr. Roberts doesn't understand my routine. Irresistibly, I think of a rider marching into a hard-to-catch horse's field, unaware of said horse's reputation, seizing said horse by the halter and leading the animal to a stall.

"What do you eat?" the dentist asks, super-seriously, after inspecting my mouth.

"Um, food?"

Lena's sitting on a chair, long legs propped up on the window seat. The office is very attractive, not antiseptic and functional like the place I usually go to. The furniture is warning me I'm going to be here a long time, so the person escorting me better relax.

"Sugar? Soda?" Dr. Roberts takes out the metallic instrument that's been picking at my mouth so I can answer him, even though I'd rather not.

"Huh?"

"Do you eat a lot of sugar and drink soda?"

"Quantify a lot," I say, thinking of the Strawberry Pop Tarts, Peanut Butter Cap' n Crunch, Mountain Dew, and takeout menus at home. I'm always determined to convince doctors and dentists how healthy I am, which I figure is almost as good as actually being healthy itself.

"How many sodas do you drink?"

"Um, two or three?"

"A week?"

"A day?" If I turn it into a question? It doesn't sound so bad?

"I'm surprised you still have teeth, frankly, much less wisdom teeth to bother you."

"I've been off my feed for a few days," I joke. He doesn't crack the tiniest bit of a grin. "The achy wisdom teeth have kept my Snickers habit under control."

He sighs. "The good news is your wisdom teeth have erupted. But you've got a lot of other stuff going on in there as well."

"Just pull them," I say. I close my eyes. "I'm not sensitive to pain."

"Then why are you clutching my chair like that?"

"I ride horses. Obviously, I'm not afraid of a little dental work." My chest feels weird and tight and my ribs are digging into the bones of my biceps.

"Simon's one of the top-ranked eventers in the country. Uncle Russell rides. Western."

"Or, as I like to call it, real riding."

"As opposed to what you and I do, Simon."

"English," he says, disdainfully. Dr. Roberts's large, powerful fingers are closer to my mouth. He's poking around in there with some silver thing. "Do you even floss?"

When he removes the pick, or whatever it is, I ask, "Do people really floss? I thought flossing was just a myth. Can't some people keep their wisdom teeth?"

"It's normal to be afraid of the dentist. But flossing is just as important as brushing."

"I'm not afraid," I say. *I ride a crazy-ass Thoroughbred no sane person would get on. I had to have a mess of nasty cancerous moles dug out of my back years ago, from years of riding and teaching in the sun. Of course, I'm not afraid of a little dental work!*

"Riding English. Not flossing," he says, shaking his head. I can see a needle in his hand. "I'm going to numb you first with the topical, before injecting the Lidocaine. Some of the greatest cowboys of the Old West were Black."

"I'm assuming they all flossed?" I ask. I become very polite at the sight of the needle, which I usually prefer to see entering a horse, not a sensitive area of my body.

"Uncle Russell, Simon doesn't want to hear your stories about the Black cowboys of the Old West. He just wants you to fix his face," says Lena.

How did they pull teeth in the Old West? I'm thinking clothesline, a slammed door, and whisky afterward to numb the pain.

Help!

"People need to know history. I don't really need to put you out completely for erupted teeth. Your teeth are actually pretty small, relative to the side of your jaw."

I don't like the fact he called my teeth small. I also feel played by the universal dentist's way of slipping into a pleasantly conversational mode, talking about everything but teeth, just before he's about to make a move. Like a chatty pickpocket.

Dr. Roberts can see I'm not fooled, so he's back to talking about my terrible teeth. "Small is a good thing. A crowded mouth is bad news, with a small jaw and large teeth. I think your wisdom teeth better come out now, so they don't cause problems later, and the general state of your oral health. It's more the grinding and wear combined that's causing the pain. The pressure from your erupted teeth compounds your problem, though."

"I'll just have the local," I say. I have horses to ride. I can't be doped up. I am absolutely not afraid of dental pain and a loss of control over this very sensitive and important part of my body. I taste the glove and the minty, sweet topical anesthetic taste. Then I feel the needle in my gum. *I am a professional horseman. I am not afraid of the dentist.*

I think I kind of pass out when the happy juice gets shot into my gum, local or no local, as I hear, but don't feel, several sickening crunches. Why does chewing Cap'n Crunch feel so satisfying, and why does this feel so shitty, even though I'm experiencing the feeling from a distance?

The next thing I can process coherently is Dr. Roberts saying it's over.

"Really? I hardly felt anything," I gasp.

"That's why Uncle Russell is the best oral surgeon in Baltimore County," says Lena, proud as if she'd done the extraction herself.

"You should have seen the wisdom teeth I extracted yesterday. Teeth beneath teeth. Decay. That patient flossed! Well, there's no justice in the world."

I ask to see the remains. I can't believe it's over. I felt nothing. When he shows me the white saber teeth with my blood and guts still hanging off of them, I nearly pass out. I'm never eating again.

As the anesthetic wears off, I become conscious of the craters I in my mouth, and the rough texture of the stitches, which he assures me will dissolve in time. Dr. Roberts tells me not to touch or rinse the wounds for twenty-four hours. Then I'm supposed to shoot water into my mouth with something that looks like some weird sex toy, to keep the wounds clean and "flushed." There's a strict schedule for reintroducing solid foods, and I get a baggie full of meds, like a junkie.

I actually feel kind of good, though. "I don't think I'll need all of these painkillers," I say, brightly.

"You're still numb. One Motrin every six hours after that, and one Vicodin every four."

"Comfortably numb. Like Pink Floyd." Maybe I am a teeny bit giddy.

"Take the day off. From the way you're grinding your teeth, I can tell you're working too hard."

"Your waiting room is full, you work hard," I point out.

"Work less. Floss more. No strenuous exercise for at least five days." He stuffs a handful of sample flosses in my goody bag. Different flavors, along with a new ultra-soft toothbrush and toothpaste for sensitive teeth. The softness and sensitivity references definitely feel... threatening on some level. I'm still bridling at the small teeth comment, even if it's a good thing he didn't have to put me under to pry out my back molars.

I notice in the waiting room on my way out, there's a photo of Dr. Roberts mounted on a big, chunky palomino. He's sporting a black cowboy hat and his black Western saddle has some tastefully glittery rhinestones embedded in it.

"I thought you said your family wasn't horsey, Lena."

"Mom isn't. My uncle got into horses because of me, actually. He loves to remind me I'm just a horse show girl, and he's a cowboy," says Lena. "Stretch out in the back seat," she says, slamming her car door behind me.

"Your uncle is very passionate about flossing," I say.

"I should have warned you. He gives out orange toothbrushes with little pumpkins and witches on them for Halloween."

"That's cold," I say.

"*Sugar is poison*," she says, imitating him.

"Tasty, delicious poison." I whip out my phone, propping myself up on my elbow. I'm having trouble forming thoughts and words, but I can read my texts, which takes less effort. "Molly messaged me that the grain shipment's full of mold and we just got a new truckload of hay. You need to take me back to the barn."

I'm convinced if I can do normal horse person things, like sling fifty-pound bales and fight with my grain guy, I'm not hurt. One part of me knows I'm being irrational. Civilians have their wisdom teeth out and rest for the day, so why shouldn't I do the same? Lena and her uncle didn't mean to hurt me. The other part of me is furious at them both, blaming them for the pain radiating from my now-not-numb jaw. I'm used to pain, but not this close to my brain. I apparently use my thinking apparatus more than I suspected in my daily routine.

"Simon, you need to go home. Seriously."

Lena goes over a pothole. I grind my remaining teeth by accident. My strength of will cracks and I take a Vicodin, slugging down the drug with one of the sealed bottles I find rolling around on the floor. The water's so warm from being in the car, I feel ill all over again. I get the Motrin down as well.

I remain curled in a C-shape in the backseat—not an easy feat for a tall man in a Toyota Camry—and eventually the world seems slippery and indeterminate, not simply because I'm in a moving car. Yet less painful. I wonder aloud why Lena has such a sensible car, hardly hearing or feeling myself speak.

"My mother bought it for me as a graduation present. She said if I was going to risk my neck riding Pilot, she was going to make sure I had the most boring, safest grandma car she could find."

At least this Toyota smells of horse, which is comforting. I use a neatly folded saddle pad I find in the back as a pillow. Lena's car is pretty clean for a horsewoman's, but there's still a bunch of pads and polo wraps lying on the floor.

Lena stops to get a coffee. She doesn't ask me if I want anything. I know nothing at Dunkin' Donuts is likely to be on an oral surgeon's master list of things I can eat. I'm also holding onto the backseat to avoid falling off.

I must be hallucinating, because as we're waiting in line, I spy Ainsley Ashcroft tripping across the asphalt in high heels. She's paired a clingy blue-and-green sequined skirt with a strappy top that leaves nothing to even my limited gay imagination of a woman's breasts. Then she's knocking on the glass with a green-lacquered fist. The other hand is holding a wristlet, one of those little clutchy purse things.

"Can I get a ride, Lena?" she asks.

This must be real, because suddenly Ainsley is sitting the passenger seat. I smell rank perfume and stale alcohol.

If this is what one painkiller does to my brain, the walls will peel and sing if I take two.

"What are you doing here, Ainsley?" asks Lena, who apparently shares my hallucination.

"I had a date. It didn't end well," says Ainsley. "I have to be back at the barn in breeches and looking human this afternoon. This is what I get for trying to dress like a real woman, not a horse trainer. Walking home from a Marriott in heels. If I'd worn my Boggs, I could have been home ages ago."

Lena orders two large coffees, just with milk for herself, and with extra cream and sugar for Ainsley. I guess Ainsley's healthy living phase is at an end, along with her time at Sandra's. When she was working for Sandra, she was ordering salads and snarfing protein bars like her slim, fashion-conscious boss.

Lena orders a bacon and cheese breakfast sandwich, hold the egg, while Ainsley asks for a cinnamon cruller and a chocolate-glazed doughnut. Soon, the car smells like coffee, melted cheese, and cinnamon sugar. I lift a finger, roll down the window, then collapse again.

"What's wrong with him? I've never seen Simon drunk before."

"Not drunk. Dentist. He just had his wisdom teeth out," says Lena.

"Really?"

"It was a pretty simple procedure. His teeth had already erupted. He's just being dramatic."

"Figures."

"My uncle had to excavate mine from my gums. He nearly passed out himself. That's why he rarely operates on family."

"I still need to get mine done when I get dental insurance. Which means I'll probably have to live with them forever. Unless I find a sugar daddy. This pony kid's dad obviously did not work out. I know I reek of the sauce, but I only had a glass of wine. I could tell from the first moment of that date I might have to bail on the sly."

The phrase "sugar daddy" seems ironic, given the lecture I just received about sugar on teeth.

"Ainsley, I thought you'd sworn off dating clients," says Lena. She sips her chaste cup of milky coffee.

"This guy took me to Applebee's, which shows you exactly what he thinks I'm worth. Fortunately, Fletch's gay, so at least I'll never be tempted by my employer." Ainsley is now talking through doughnut.

Everything they say about Vicodin is correct, because I'm not even hungry, despite not having eaten today, and I don't feel annoyed at Ainsley through the fog. I know my mouth is still in pain, but I feel the pain from a distance. I'm observing myself. Suddenly, I don't care about anything, I just run my tongue over my stitched wounds as the car speeds out of the drive-thru.

Ainsley made resolutions to clean herself up. She's drinking less than she used to, but still making bad dating decisions. *People don't change.* That's why I'm not making any resolutions about improving my dental health. I'm not pretending I'm going to become one of those people who leaps out of bed, proclaiming it's a great day for flossing.

"I heard you'd given up riding, Lena," asks Ainsley. "Then I heard you were switching over to eventing. What is it?" Ainsley, unlike myself, has a talent for unearthing all the latest gossip. She's in interrogation mode. I'm a little surprised at how unsubtle she is. But it works. Most people love to talk about themselves.

Even tight-lipped Lena seems to appreciate the opportunity to mull over her thoughts with someone who won't encourage her to ride one of his horses as a solution to fix her feelings. Also, Ainsley's life is always such a trash fire, by comparison anyone else's seems better. Having a friend or frenemy like that can be a comfort. Ainsley is unshockable.

"I've basically given up ever since I had to sell Pilot and leave Vince's."

"But what are you doing with Simon?" I realize both women think I've passed out cold. I open my eyes a slit to see Ainsley delicately licking cinnamon sugar from the sparkly green polish on her fingernails. Then I crinkle my lids shut. The light is painful. The saddle pad is comfortable.

"I'm studying for my SATs and I'm going to apply to college for next year. Simon sucked me into his orbit."

I hide a snort of laughter in the saddle pad I'm resting on.

"He does that. Jelly, frankly. Of leaving the horse world, I mean, not jelly of the fact you've got Simon drooling on your saddle pads in the backseat."

I'm going to kill Ainsley, I think. But the thought feels very distant. Like a cartoon bubble hanging in the air.

"Oh, Ainsley, you'll never tire of it. You're not like me."

"Riding for Mackenzie didn't help your perspective. You need to ride for someone sane."

"You rode with Wilson, who was just as bad. Mackenzie never tried anything with me. Guess I wasn't cute enough."

"Or he was scared of your mom."

"That too. You see, after Paula, my mother was always very protective."

"Shit, that's right, you started with Paula Kirkpatrick."

Lena takes out a tiny ketchup packet, squeezes the contents on the bun of her sandwich as she steadies the wheel with her knees. She then reassembles the sandwich, eats it one-handed, wrapper in her lap to catch any crumbs. She doesn't get a smear of grease or condiment on herself or the wheel.

"I was so ignorant back then, and so was my mom. Paula took full advantage," says Lena.

"I'll bet. I've heard the stories."

"You don't know the half of it. I started training with her when I was twelve. When I was fourteen, she asked me to be her full-time working student. As in, come to work at the barn all day for free while still paying full price for lessons and training for my horse. I got caught up in the glory of riding for the A-circuit showjumping queen."

Ainsley snorts. "The only reason Paula won so much was because of the nice horses she conned off of the rich ladies riding for her. The Paula Cult."

"I got sucked into the Cult, only worse, because I was her unpaid employee. Her 'barn rat.' 'You're a barn rat, just like I was at your age, Lena,' she'd say, and I'd be glowing for days. *I was just like her!* Suddenly, I was giving lessons—lessons—to grown-ass adults. She called me her 'Assistant Trainer' but never paid me a thing. In fact, she charged me for the training rides I gave to the green horses or I rode in lessons and charged the owners for training. They thought she was riding them, not some kid. I don't think my adult students knew I was a freshman in high school. That was back when I was still going to school school, versus online high school."

"Paula was usually less than sober, so you probably did a better job," says Ainsley. Lena turns up the air-conditioning, since the midday sun is getting hotter. I move closer, hand shielding my face, to hear over the cooling roar. I know of Paula Kirkpatrick, and I love a good Paula story.

"I was so naïve at fourteen, I didn't even understand she was drunk most of the time. I thought that was just her way."

"That's why, if someone is a truly functional alcoholic, it's better if they keep topping up, so people never see the difference."

"Once, I remember finding a half-finished plastic Solo cup of wine in the tack room, near the white show pads. I tossed it, because I was afraid those pads would get dirty. I thought the cup was full of funky grape juice or flat soda, because it smelled funny. When she found out, I was sure she was going to tie my horse to the fence that day and kick us both out."

"Red wine? Now that was sloppy. I think during shows she'd just do the vodka-in-the-Diet Coke-can trick, or white wine in an iced tea bottle."

"You remember how I went through that bad patch with Leo, my first horse. Paula would tell me not to warm up without her. Then, she wouldn't show until I had to compete, so there I'd be, with no practice, no one to go over the course properly. Which I was paying for, or rather, my mom was paying for. I was jumping poor old Leo cold at shows. Because of her!"

"Your mom didn't read her the riot act?"

"Mama knows nothing about horses, and then, in my eyes, Paula could do no wrong. I'd always defend Paula, say poor Paula was being worked to death by her clients. I felt I was the only one who understood what poor Paula was going through. Paula used me as her therapist. Told me stuff about her current boyfriend, her exes. Stuff I didn't need to hear. She treated me more like someone her own age. But Paula let me ride all of her best horses, including Alfonzo."

"Oh yeah, The Fonz! I remember him. Big bay, white socks, blaze."

"He had such a soft mouth."

"No thanks to Paula."

"Was always in front of my leg."

This conversation would mean something very different, if it wasn't being had by two horse girls. I hold on to the seat tight while my stomach lurches with the motion of the car. Lena rolls up the window to keep the air-conditioning in. The smell of food gets stronger.

Lena continues: "I knew if I complained, I'd lose them all. My mother worried about me because I'd lost a ton of weight. Paula never gave me time for lunch breaks. Or dinner breaks. I felt guilty about feeling hungry and not putting the horse's needs first. Like, once Paula told me not to stop walking her colicking horse. No money for the vet, of course, although she always had money for new saddles and wine. I was walking for hours.

"There was this tiny little bag of Doritos and one of those six-packs of Oreos sitting on a chair and I just kept walking and walking this poor horse, praying and praying he'd give up the ghosts in his guts and poop. Fantasizing about that food. I reached out and grabbed one chip after I was sure I was going to pass out, and I heard, from nowhere, 'I see you Lena. Do you want that horse to die because you needed a Dorito?' I was so scared! I was like, 'Lord, she's everywhere. I'm going to kill her poor horse.' Fortunately, the horse ended up fine. I did not.

"That was during the winter—oh yeah, did I mention I worked seven days, weekends and after school for her—and I caught the flu. Although I was so achy from working, it was hard to tell. I went into school and still kept working. The horses needed me! Paula's business would go under if it wasn't for me! She'd convinced me the horses would all starve if I slacked off. The weight of the barn rested on my boney little shoulders. I admit, I kind of got a high from it. No other kid I knew had the responsibility of an entire barn. Mom and Uncle Russell staged an intervention and tried to talk sense into me, but I was so bullheaded, I wouldn't hear of it. I kept my grades up, so they couldn't complain. I lied about how much work I was actually doing, and how often Paula was there."

Cold weather and many a horse's fondness for going on water strikes is a great way for the intestines to get sluggish and blocked. A fact I know all too well, just like how I know even a decent rider will often stick with a bad trainer if said trainer has access to nice horses.

"It was when Paula went to Germany for a week to compete and look at sale horses and left me in charge, I got pushed to the edge. This was in the summer, at least, so I wasn't in school, and I wasn't dealing with frozen hoses. She said, 'You know the horse's feeding schedule, you can teach the lessons that week, and most people are away on vacation.' Which was true. But she still left a fifteen-year-old in charge of an entire show barn! I was so scared!"

"Did she pay you? Anything?"

"Of course not! Looking back, it was hilarious. Like these fancy clients were blowing up my phone, asking about their horses, and talking to little high school me. A German guy called. I remember saying, quite seriously, because I couldn't understand his accent, 'Excuse me, sir, could you be a little less German?' He wanted to know if she was still interested in breeding her mares and talked frozen semen versus live cover. I was thinking, 'I'm not sure I'm even old enough to have this conversation.' Not that I hadn't cleaned all the sheaths of Paula's geldings by then."

"Semen or live cover? What did you say?"

"I said, 'there's always a risk to the mare with live cover that you don't have with frozen, so Ms. Kirkpatrick might be interested.'"

"How did you pull that one out of your skinny ass? Because it's true."

"I rose to the occasion, Ainsley, I rose," says Lena.

"Was she thinking of breeding one of her mares? All of her mares were as crazy as she was."

"I don't know. She was looking into everything to make money. There's this farm over here that has like a whole freezer full of European horse semen."

"Like flavors of ice cream?"

"It's funny, I was so over my head, and didn't even realize it. When you're a teenager, you don't know what you don't know. Managing that circus by myself now would scare me more than when I was a kid."

"It's kind of nice how, when you're fourteen or fifteen, you think you know everything. I never worried I'd hurt myself when I was a kid."

"It wasn't until school started up again, and Paula was actually encouraging me to cut class to help her out at the barn, that my mom pulled the plug on the ATM. Plus, I was as tall as I am now, and about ninety-eight pounds, tops, because Paula never gave me time to eat. I once passed out in school. From walking in the hallway, not even riding. Honestly, after what happened to me with Pilot and the concussion I got in school, if I hurt my head again, my brain is toast."

"Shit, Lena, I'm so sorry," says Ainsley. "I was really lucky I found Liv. I'll never ride for another owner like her."

"Liv had money, Paula didn't, that's the difference. I don't come from enough money, either. The reason I was so desperate to please Paula in the first place was because it was during a bad patch for my mom, during the few years they wrote her off *Riverview*. We were living off her concert and stage money. You should have heard Paula when I told her I was switching barns."

"I can imagine."

"'You're so ungrateful! After what I've done for you! You'll never ride at my level again! You're going nowhere in this industry!' And worst of all, 'You're a quitter.'" Lena does a pinched, nasal imitation of a voice that shows she's an actress's daughter, despite her denials of having any talent in that area.

Then she sobers. "It was the word 'quitter' that hurt. I vowed I wasn't a quitter. A quitter doesn't walk a horse with colic in a dark arena until four in the morning on a cold winter Sunday! The fear of being a quitter is why I never gave up on Pilot, even after everyone told me he didn't have the brain to be a consistent winner."

"That horse nearly killed you, Lena," says Ainsley. "He was trying to kill his riders for years. You know I speak the truth."

"I thought he was trying to kill me a little less, though, less than some of his previous riders! After Paula, my uncle took me aside and told me to be like him, have a little hobbyhorse farm, but a real job."

As far as I'm concerned, a dentist is *too* real of a job.

The next thing I hear is Lena saying, "All horse pros are crazy. Simon? Simon? You're home."

"I'll help Molly unload the hay, and she can drive me home," I say to Lena through the fog. "Plus, I need to figure out the grain situation."

"We're not at the barn. We're at your house-home, not your barn home. Ainsley and I are helping your barn manager with the chores today," says Lena firmly.

"Ainsley's in a dress," I mutter.

"Why, how surprisingly kind and gentlemanly of you to notice, Simon. You must be on lots of drugs. But there's a spare pair of boots I can throw on at the barn, I'm sure," says Ainsley. "I can borrow Molly's. Your barn manager is there, right?"

"Lena, it's not your responsibility. Or Ainsley's. Or Molly's. It's my barn! O' Shaughnessy Eventing!"

"You're a friend. You let me ride your horse, and I made you go to the oral surgeon. You can only have all your wisdom teeth out once, so you might as well enjoy it. Go home. Watch TV. Let someone else take care of you," says Lena.

"Eric's teaching summer school at St. Augustine's. He's busy." I don't want to move. I don't want to go home. I feel uneasy, leaving other people to do my work. I don't want to pull a Paula, though I'm only hiding away for an afternoon in my bed, not on the Continent.

Then I black out. Sort of. I can hear voices, but can't really respond. Too much effort.

"Is he always *like this*, Ainsley?"

"Like what? He's doped up on more meds than a show hunter, Lena."

"My uncle just ripped four teeth out of his head and he wants to unload grain and hay."

"Oh yeah, Simon's always like that. That's not the drugs."

I manage to finagle my way out of Lena's car and find my way to my front door. Time seems pretty elastic right now, kind of like my joints. I locate my key and let myself in. Then, I lie down on the couch, text Eric I'm home, put my phone in a place I won't fall asleep on and crush it, and turn on the television. It's tuned to network TV, and finding something to stream seems too complicated now.

This is the first time I've watched a long stretch of daytime television. I know kids used to fake sick so they could watch reruns or soaps. I never wanted to, because it would mean missing out on horse time. Hell, my mom used to give me permission to skip school if we were getting a hay delivery at the barn where she taught, and they needed some extra hands. But lying around in front of a screen with ginger ale and cookies on a tray was not Mom's style. Sicking out from school just meant having to do a different kind of work.

I discover I'm actually pretty good guessing *The Price Is Right*. Who knew?

The fact I'm on my couch while Lena, Ainsley, and Molly are with my horses is eating into me. Eating into me like this guy is tucking into a Red Lobster all-you-can-eat shrimp festival in this commercial. Then, I'm really sure I'm hallucinating again, as I see Lena on the screen, right after the shrimp. It takes a beat to realize I'm watching *Riverview General*.

"You can't push me around! I've been here since you were playing doctor in the bushes, young man." The doctor Lena is talking to grins so brashly, even I want to punch his face. Suddenly, I register this isn't Lena, but Lena's mom.

Because I don't really trust myself to move very much, I watch. I'd like to read the latest paranormal fantasy I've downloaded to my phone (because of the shirtless guy on the cover). This is, I assure you, completely different from

70

weirdo medieval cosplay. But I think too many words on a screen will make me nauseous.

I can see Serena St. Claire's nostrils flaring beneath her contouring, or whatever they call that blush, the kind that makes your cheekbones look high. The bat wings of her eyelids are visible even through my gauzy Vicodin and Motrin haze.

My phone rings. I have to move. A horse could be dead. Lena, Molly, and Ainsley are at the barn right now. Anything could be happening.

"This is Serena St. Claire," I hear. Her voice is creamy, enunciated, and even more correct than she sounds on the television.

I drop my phone. I pick it up again, and clear the cotton wool enough from my brain not to say, "But you're on TV!"

"I understand you're my daughter's new coach, or trainer, or whatever you horse people call them." From Lena's story, I know that her mom probably knows a bit more about horses than this, but she's emphasizing her ignorance as a sign of disgust.

"No, no. Lena's just a friend I've taken riding a few times," I say. Great, that sounds like a euphemism for something else. "You'll have to excuse me. I just had wisdom tooth surgery. Or rather, teeth surgery. I'm a little loopy." High as a helium balloon, more like it.

"I don't consider someone a friend who takes my daughter riding on a dangerous horse."

"The horse is not dangerous!" I can't believe she's calling my Owen crazy, after what Lena was riding for years. "Doesn't Lena's uncle ride?" Uncle Russell should understand.

"Oh, my brother the *cowboy*."

"There's always risk with riding horses, but I took care of Lena as best as I knew how."

"I will speak to Lena later. I've had to play my own evil twin all this week. Double my usual lines. It's been hectic."

I hope she doesn't get in touch with Lena while Lena's unloading hay for me.

After Lena's mom hangs up, I check to see what the women at my barn are up to, scrolling to the barn's Instagram rather than texting Molly. I don't feel like talking. Molly always talks, even when she has nothing to say.

Molly has taken a short video. Ainsley is in her evening dress and stockings, wearing a pair of too-big Boggs boots that come almost up over her knees, standing on top of a mound of hay. She's throwing bales of hay to Lena, who is covering her head and running away.

I lay back on my pillow. Hay Tetris. Pretty much what I expected. People are destroying the little dignity I still possess on social media.

I hear the doorbell ring about a half hour, maybe two hours later? What is time? By now, *Riverview General* has been long over.

"Eric!" My boyfriend is still in his work clothes of a yellow tie, and a natty blue Oxford button-down shirt.

"How are you feeling? I worried about you all day. I've bought some soft foods."

I collapse on the couch. "I'm fine."

"You look like death. Here's a milkshake." He turns off the television. "What are you watching?"

I suck the plastic straw and a hit of vanilla and peanut butter bypasses my aching teeth and hits my brain.

"I don't even know. This is a sexy beast of a milkshake," I say, and pull myself up slightly to show the intensity of my affection. Now that I'm getting some serious calories in me, I feel less peaked. I'm sure the milkshake has sugar, but there's no way to juice or blend a steak. "I was just speaking with Serena St. Claire," I say, and flop back down to my prone position. I snuggle closer to Eric's thigh to show my appreciation for his efforts, although I don't trust myself to grab said muscular thigh, because I think I need two hands to steady my shake.

"What? You mean you were watching her on TV?" He rests his hand on my forehead. I love this man. I'd have a hard-on for him and his milkshake if I weren't so exhausted, doped up, and sore. Even kissing, with my mouth as it is right now, is a big ol' no bueno.

"No, no, Lena Roberts is Serena St. Claire's daughter. You know, Lena, who I ride with sometimes. Her mom called me."

"Oh my God," he says, and withdraws his hand. "I saw Serena three times on Broadway alone. I have the soundtracks of every musical she's ever appeared in. Her daughter rides?"

I return his cool fingers to my hot forehead. I need it there to keep me from falling off the face of the earth. Serena St. Claire has already maxed out my limits of conversation for today. I close my eyes. "I thought Serena was a soap star."

"That's only what people who know *nothing* about *the theater* say." I've offended Eric. He says *theater* so prayerfully. The fact I am just gay, but not Theater Gay, is now painfully clear.

I pull myself up to sitting, put down my precious milkshake and Eric massages my shoulders. I touch my chin to my chest.

I jerk my head up, suddenly aware of how much time has passed if Eric's finished work. "I better give Molly a call to make sure she's doing okay."

"Don't worry, I stopped over before I came here. I knew you'd be thinking more about the barn than your own health."

I put my milkshake on the side table and stand. Nope, probably not a good idea. The ground feels spongy; I slide into the welcoming fold of sofa, my head once again on Eric's thighs.

"Simon, you've just had your wisdom teeth out. Rest."

"Horses don't rest, so I don't rest."

"Take another sip of your shake."

I check the time. It's been four hours, so I take my second Vicodin, washing it down with the shake. "Eric? I have a personal question."

He pauses.

"Do I eat too much sugar?"

"Define too much."

"Do you floss, Eric?"

"Of course!"

"I always thought flossing was a myth. Something people talked about but never really did, like using a pea-sized amount of toothpaste on the brush."

"Do you think you'll be well enough to go to the Renaissance Faire with me this weekend?"

"I agreed to go with you to the Renaissance Faire?"

"You didn't *disagree*."

Despite the misery my mouth is giving me, I am hungry. The thick, sweet shake Eric bought me does, I admit, taste pretty good. He gives me a napkin to wrap around the beaded, damp plastic cup. In two hours, I'm due for a Motrin. I can hold out until then.

These are good arguments for going along with what he says, to make him happy.

Still.

"You know those people in the weird costumes nearly killed Lena?"

"The people doing LARP didn't mean to take the horse by surprise. I'm sure these aren't the same folks. Lots of locals work at the Faire."

"I don't think I'll be up to it."

"You're not riding tomorrow?"

"Of course, I'm riding tomorrow."

"How can you be well enough to ride tomorrow, but not well enough to go to the Faire with me this weekend?"

Christ on a cracker. "What is this, some kind of debate or something? Those are completely different activities."

"How?"

"One requires a lot more emotional effort!"

"I don't think you're supposed to exercise after wisdom tooth surgery."

"The surgeon said nothing strenuous for five days. So, not jumping anything big, you know?"

Eric sighs.

I remind myself how Eric has helped me out with the horses many times, despite being afraid of horses. That he's my boyfriend, and I do like spending time with him. The meaner part of me says things involving horses are necessary, and going to a Renaissance Faire is the exact opposite of necessary.

When Eric is in the bathroom, his phone lights up. I can't stop myself. His prickly reaction whenever I touch it makes me want to seize it, like a child poking fingers into the frosting of a newly decorated cake. Or a fire.

There's a message from a number I don't recognize. A tiny black-and-white acting headshot of Dylan Clarke's photograph hangs over said number.

4pm tomorrow works.

I hunt and peck around on the phone, but can't find a clue what this conversation refers to; I even check to see if

Eric has reinstalled Grindr or some other dating app on his phone. He hasn't.

I debate bringing up the text. Can I admit I didn't trust him enough *not* to invade his privacy? But he's back to rubbing my neck. I sip my shake, not wanting to know just now what it all means, because I'm too drugged and sore, despite having done nothing more productive all day than lose teeth. I haven't even ridden any horses.

Chapter 4
A Renaissance of Learning

"Gentlemen! Hast thou heard the news of King Henry's fetching young strumpet?"

Normally, I don't notice a woman's cleavage, but this woman has hiked her breasts up so high in her corset-thing, her silver cross is practically buried in her flesh. The legs of Jesus are drawing my eye to the V.

"But hark! I do hear the traveling troubadours are coming this way. Make haste, make haste, and list." The serving wench skips away, her long burlap skirt swishing.

"This Renaissance Faire isn't as big as the Maryland Renaissance Festival," Eric says, lamely, touching my bare arm as if that makes everything around us less medieval. Or Renaissance. Did they torture during the Renaissance? Because this is torture. "Why not relax and try to have fun?" Eric asks. "Look, they're selling silver skull rings over there. You love little skulls, Simon!" He gently steers me, using my elbow as a rudder, to the tent.

"You promised me men wearing kilts," I say. There is a distinct absence of muscular calves under kilts and a distinct abundance of serving wenches.

"Can I help you with anything?" asks the woman sitting on a canvas chair at the jewelry booth. Unlike most of the other people I've encountered at the Faire, she's not using a fake British accent. Though she sounds pretty uptight. I think she overheard my comments about kilts. Thanks to my career as a riding instructor, I have no indoor voice. Or even a slightly muted outdoor voice for a venue like this.

The rings are too cutesy for my taste, all little sparkly crystal balls and wizards. Eric seems to be enjoying himself, so I try to be less sulky. Winning a stuffed beaver at the axe-throwing tent improves my mood slightly. I get some applause from the beefy guys who failed to lodge the hatchet in the lumber. I hit the target every time. Despite my mother's cruel denial of video games when Sean and I were kids—my mom was very into "fresh air," including the "fresh air" of cleaning stalls—I've always had excellent hand-to-eye coordination.

"If you'd just relax, I bet you might have fun," murmurs Eric.

I put my arm around Eric's waist. I like the way his warm, solid body feels pressed into mine. I give him the stuffed animal to hold with his opposite arm.

A lady navigating an elaborate contraption of a stroller over the dirt paths gives us a dirty look. Eric subtly withdraws from my clasp, still clutching the beaver.

Now who's the one not relaxing? It's bad enough I have to deal with The Straights, much less with kids, at family-friendly events like horse trials. Why must I seek them out? My arm curls up around Eric, where it should be, again. A tribe of high school students enfolds us. The kids are in black t-shirts and Goth makeup, as well as a couple cosplaying in Renaissance gear. The change in the appearance and mood of the crowd pacifies me. Slightly. As does a plastic cup of icy beer.

The winding dirt paths have cute names like Ye Olde Tavern Lane and Executioner's Rowe. When we turn down one of them, we're greeted by a guy in full armor wielding a hatchet. "Ye shall not pass. Do you bite your thumb at me?"

"I don't even floss," I say.

Just then, a miniature horse wearing a red-and-white saddle blanket and a halter decorated with red roses trots by. "Loose horse!" I hear.

I have to stifle a laugh. I grab the lead rope trailing from the mini's halter easily. Suddenly, he swings a kick in my direction. At me, a professional horseman. I'm holding onto a postage stamp-sized horse decked out like a birthday cake.

"Who does he belong to?" I ask, looking around.

"The living chess match," says Eric. "I remember the knights with miniature horses from last year."

On one square of the large chessboard they've set up in a field, there's a very sad-looking knight, trying to do his best to go on with the show, horseless. He rather unenthusiastically takes the little white horse I offer to him in hand. I look at the little black miniature horse on the other side, who is also being led by a man in a knight's costume. None of the other pieces are being played by animals, thank God.

I rejoin Eric. "The knights aren't even mounted."

"I suppose a real-sized horse wouldn't fit on a square."

"Still, weak!"

The enthroned king is playing red. The queen is white, and they say their moves aloud, on a microphone, so we all can hear them.

I remember the pleasure I used to take beating my old boyfriend Max at chess, and how I played the game with my father when he was in the hospital, dying. The closed, focused, emotionless bubble of a logic game usually comforts me. This spectacle is just ridiculous. Knowing how to play chess and ride actual horses makes the sight annoy me all the more.

"Is there something about you that attracts animals on the loose?" Eric asks.

"Animal magnetism? Well, I won you a stuffed beaver, not a horse." This sounds vaguely obscene. "Is there jousting here? Because if there is, I want to see the jousting." I'm joking, of course, but someone selling Morgan Le Fay's Fairy

Cakes from a tray stops and says there is, in fact, jousting at noon.

The jousting is a *production*, with guys in pastel tights blowing horns to summon us all and a different queen walking hand-in-hand with the actor kitted up to look like Henry VIII, versus the generic-looking king playing chess. I guess this queen is the one he didn't behead. Heavy draft horses wear breastplates, flags dangling from the reins, and the knights sit in comfy black dressage saddles.

It's hard to tell how much is spontaneous or choreographed, but the lumbering horses know their jobs, and put on a pretty credible demonstration as their riders *argh* and *ugh*, clashing with one another, crashing their lances. The queen touches the shoulders of the winning champion with a flat, dull sword.

Eric's applause is unreasonably loud.

"You never clap after I ride," I say.

"Yes, but I actually kind of understand what they're doing."

"What don't you understand about my riding?"

"I understand about staying on and going fast. I don't understand the technical stuff."

"Like what?"

"Like dressage."

"I'm not sure even I understand dressage, Eric."

I'm not joking. To a civilian non-rider, dressage appears to be nothing but a tedious series of endless circles and adjustments of three gaits. To an eventer with the right horse for cross-country and the wrong horse for dressage, the discipline's language of relaxation, suppleness, and effortless effort seems like witchcraft.

How is it that what I do—spontaneous, with a high level of risk involved, an actual sport—evokes confusion, fear, or, worst of all, indifference in the minds of most civilians, including my boyfriend? Take a cart horse, put his rider in armor, give the rider a lance and hang flags on his saddle, and Eric's impressed. This is the only interest he's shown in horses I can remember. "Let's go introduce ourselves backstage," I say. Back tent.

One knight is already stripping himself of his armor, while a woman in a serving wench costume holds the horse. She doesn't look happy about it. The horse is glistening with sweat.

"That jousting was, um, a lot," I say, trying to sound admiring and put into words what Eric evidentially feels. "I ride horses myself. Simon O' Shaughnessy. I run an eventing barn nearby." I feel like I'm throwing down a glove or a gauntlet, or whatever those old-time knights used to challenge one another.

"I'm Callum Rudd." Like Eric, Knight Callum has no discernable body hair, not even my blond fuzz. He's pasty and pale as the burnout guys I used to have lunch with in the cafeteria. Unlike Eric (who is a runner and has zero upper body tone), he's jacked from the waist up. I'm guessing it's from wearing the armor as much as the swordplay itself. Or maybe he just CrossFits when he's not being all medieval. "Eventing, that's jumping, right?"

He's affecting deliberate stupidity. "I can't believe you're a Marylander who rides and has never tried eventing," I say.

"Jousting is the official sport of Maryland," Callum adds, as if that makes it super-butch. "Have you ever jousted?"

"Eventing takes up a lot of time."

"So does jousting."

"Eventing has three separate phases!" I feel pathetic, like the people who tell me they know how to ride because they went on a trail ride once. One reason Eric endears himself to me, despite being a civilian, is the fact he's never pretended he could ride, and admits he fell off when he tried to learn at summer camp.

Fortunately, Callum puts on a black t-shirt over his ripped chest so I don't stare too much in front of my boyfriend. Even the open-flapped tent is rank with steamy, stinking air from the bodies of horses and men. Callum picks up a bucket, and gently pours the water upon the glistening horse, sponges the animal's black back, and then sweat-scrapes off the moisture. There is an element of showboating at how easily he picks up the heavy bucket, as well as how quietly the horse stands with the cotton lead rope hanging off the shoulder.

I think of how Morrissey would sidestep away from me and the water, if he were here instead. Especially when Callum's haphazardly stacked armor makes a clattering sound as it falls from its pile to the earth, as a breeze wafts in through the tent. The hot, inland wind blowing in makes things hotter, rather than cooler.

The gold armor looks familiar, and suddenly it registers. "You! You're the one who attacked my horse at the horse park."

"I remember a Black girl riding a horse going crazy."

"My horse. Who is not crazy. My friend. Who is a very accomplished rider."

"Is she?"

The way he describes Lena, I don't know, it just rubs me the wrong way. I guess it's not factually wrong, but it feels wrong, the way he's saying it. I stick to the relevant facts. "You don't go after a scared horse like that."

"I understand. It's not every rider who can train his horse like mine. Bailey can deal with crowds, screaming kids, you name it. So can Bobby Joe, Sam's horse," he says, gesturing to his beefy blond friend, who is sponging off a hairy, drafty paint with heavily feathered legs. "I've jousted, even marched in parades with Bailey. I've taken him LARP-ing. That's Live Action Role Playing, you know."

Callum is lucky I'm with Eric, as Eric will kill me if I try to kill this man. "I've desensitized my horses to a lot, but some have their quirks. You don't get in a horse's face like that, not with any of mine, ever again. If you're in a horse park, doing… whatever you people were doing… you respect there may be horses there, green horses, inexperienced riders. Not every horse is a parade horse. You don't run screaming all over the place like maniacs."

"LARP-ing," says Callum.

"LARP-ing," I say, through gritted, painful teeth. I run my tongue over my stitches. Dr. Roberts said they'd dissolve, eventually. I try to hasten the process and take out my aggression against the world by rubbing them with my tongue constantly.

Sam, other jouster, tells Callum to pack up their gear. Eric and I leave.

I'm steaming more than the big jousting horses. I hate having anything horse-related I don't know about rubbed in my face. I can't deny it takes a certain amount of skill to desensitize even a quiet draft cross to crowds, noise, and heavy tack. I feel I've failed as a trainer.

"His horse seemed like a very kind horse," says Eric.

I'm still grinding my teeth.

"Even though his rider was a dick," adds Eric.

My jaw is in pain, I'm clenching it so hard.

"Take a breath, Simon."

I put my hand on Eric's shoulder and give him a squeeze. Despite being a theater guy, Eric works at Catholic school, and he's never been physically demonstrative with me in public. The fact I'm in my stupid black t-shirt and jeans in this heat further fouls my mood. I should have learned my lesson at Barb's and worn something lighter. Something I can breathe in. Even my skin is smothering.

A tiny girl walks by with a Flintstone-sized turkey drumstick. "Those drumsticks are the only reason I agreed to come here."

"Simon, your teeth. Or where your teeth once were. Aren't you supposed to be eating soft foods?"

"What did medieval people eat when their teeth hurt? Porridge? Beer?" I ask.

"Probably just died of starvation."

Trust Eric to always say even a more morbid fucking thing than myself.

"So why are we celebrating this period of history at this Faire thing, again?"

Eric has to stop at a Porta-Potty and gives me his phone and the stuffed beaver to hold. He's clumsy and is afraid he'll drop one or the other.

I can't resist. I know the passcode. I check his messages again. Dylan Clarke has left him more texts, and Eric has responded.

Dylan's little bubble reads: *We could meet on Tuesday or Thursday afternoon, your call.*

Tuesday works, Eric has responded.

4pm? asks the Dylan bubble.

Great, looking forward to it, Eric wrote.

I don't understand. There's nothing about Eric's demeanor that suggests he's cheating on me. Have I grown that shitty at reading not only Owen's body language but also my boyfriend's? I remember Ben Hillard, an eventer I used to sort of date years ago. He cheated on me, seemingly out of nowhere. Eric's a former actor. He's a professional pretender. Why wouldn't he mention this guy to me? There may be some innocent explanation, although I can't think of one.

I remember all the times Eric has been so honest with me. About his fear of horses, living with his parents, even his failure to make it as an actor. I call the number and Dylan's voicemail picks up, just a message with his name and a request to leave a message. I don't, of course.

Eric returns.

"I'm determined to feast on some turkey drumsticks from King Henry's Ye Olde Tavern, teeth or no teeth," I say. I hand back his phone but cling to the stuffed beaver. "I'm thinking of naming this furry guy Dylan," I blurt out, trying to catch Eric by surprise.

But Eric doesn't react like a man who just heard his boyfriend say the name of his secret lover. "He looks more like a Bucky to me, but you've more experience naming animals."

The turkey is smoky, falling off the bone into my greedy gnawing teeth, although I wonder where they find so many freakishly large turkeys with pumped up legs. Is there, like, carnage at some turkey gyms waged by the Faire cooks? I wash the gristle and dark meat of the meat lollypop out of my stitches with my little plunger (which I have to keep in my pocket at all times, like an asshole), then we go a-hunting for some of ye funnel cake and hard lemonade.

"To Dr. Russell Roberts, master oral surgeon," I say, clinking transparent plastic cups with Eric, "Without whom chewing this meal would not be possible."

On the ride home, Eric tires of my teasing, jabbing barbs about the Faire. "Do you have to be so contemptuous?" His SAT word makes me even grumpier. "Fantasy books and drama kept me going through a dark place in my teenage life, once upon a time. I thought you liked *Star Wars*, Simon."

"*Star Wars* is a completely different animal!"

"There's swordplay in *Star Wars*!"

"They're called light sabers, Eric." I whip out my phone and start surfing.

"Simon, if you need to use your phone, let me drive," says Eric. "I'm the faculty advisor for a club specifically dedicated to persuading kids not to text behind the wheel."

"I'm looking for jousting lessons," I say.

"I was afraid of that," Eric says. He takes my phone away from me, gently. "You won't beat Callum in a joust with a couple of lessons."

"I won't?"

"Why is everything a competition with you? Be the bigger person and just walk away."

Christ on a cracker. Or Christ on a cheap silver pendant between some medieval serving wench's breasts.

"I'm sorry you hated Faire so much. Thanks for coming with me, anyway."

"I didn't mean it like that, Eric! I didn't exactly hate it. I don't know, I just felt dumb. It seemed, well, cheesy."

"I know the Faire is kind of kitschy, but I just like a bit of theater and history in my life. Is that so terrible?"

I feel like a monster.

Eric flicks through the sound system, settles on something that sounds like a Broadway show tune, and sings. I know he's trying to change the subject. "You have an incredible voice," I say, surprised, because I've never really heard him belt out a song before, not like this. My ex-boyfriend Max used to be in a band and could sing way better than me, but Eric is in a different league.

"I have an okay voice."

"I still think you should give acting another go," I say.

"What? In New York? Leave my students? Leave you? Since when did you care about acting?"

"I'm not saying I want you to leave me. Don't get all prickly-weird like you sometimes do." I feel on some level

Eric knows he's wasting something, his musical gift, but can't bear to take the risk of failing again. "I feel bad you miss it so much."

"I know I'm talented." The way he says it, it's not arrogant, but kind of flat and bitter. "But I'm not marketable as a 'type.' I couldn't find work. It's not that I don't love it enough," he says, with the lightness that comes into his voice only when he's talking about something very serious and trying to avoid an argument.

I squeeze his hand, waiting for a red light to scroll through a few more webpages about jousting. The phone is resting right near the cup holder of my Subaru; I can see it trembling with the motion of the car.

I'd get angry when my teachers said I was wasting my potential at the barn and should go to college. I think Eric is wasting his potential as a teacher, hiding behind a desk. A desk in front of a whiteboard. Just the idea of desks, sitting, makes me want to run.

I want to know more about this Dylan guy. I feel like I'm an open book, and he should be the same.

"I wonder what that guy Callum does for a living," I muse aloud. "I mean, it's not possible to be a professional jouster, is it?"

"Probably something really boring, like a librarian or a history teacher," says Eric.

"You're a history teacher."

"Exactly."

"Shut up," I say, and squeeze Eric's knee.

I don't really care how dull Callum might be outside of his horsey life. I know I'm 0-2 against him. Faire prize beaver or no beaver strapped in the back seat. I want to win a perfectly behaved horse. Even if it kills me.

Chapter 5
Several Fries Short of a Happy Meal

I bridge my reins, make the braided leather taunt over Morrissey's neck, lighten my seat in my already-short stirrups, and let my horse fly.

It's six in the morning. I muttered to the woman at the McDonald's drive-thru something about beating the heat, when she asked why I was up so early. My wounds are healing, so when I plunge and spit, I excavate less pus and remnants of food with every meal.

Fried potato hash browns and sticky sweet soda, chased down by an egg and cheese biscuit in the car. My stomach is regretting that hash brown right now, though.

Riding, no one can see my crooked, sore mouth beneath my helmet, or my checkered history. To an outsider, Morrissey and I are the picture of the perfect rider and Thoroughbred. I am in my worn half-chaps and skullcap. He is sweating and frothing in the steaming mists of the morning. But as free as we appear, we are not unlike an office worker or a racehorse; I must keep my eye on the clock. My luminescent stopwatch tells me how many meters per minute we must race.

We appear to be racing nothing. Yet we are trying to outpace our older, lesser selves. I am told that eventing prepares a horse for battle. This is a more subtle, uncomfortable tussle between horse and rider than jousting. Stride by stride, jump by jump, we wage a merry war. We should be allies, yet we are neither friends nor enemies. We constantly question one another, agree to disagree. Little lover's spats over obstacles.

Morrissey is a horse who has thrown me and injured me badly. He's also a horse I won Jersey Fresh on, a major event. He's a horse I restarted after he raced on the track, who I know as well as my own hand, the hand he stepped on. He's a horse who I'm still uncertain about taking abroad, to Badminton or Burghley, to test him against the biggest of big tracks, though it was with that intention I bought him.

I feel satisfied at the end of our schooling. Morrissey is sweating, but amped up by the dizzying heat more than wearied by it. We walk a long time, and never really cool off, just transition from hot steam to cold sweat. I'll give him a proper bath back at the barn.

Driving the trailer home, I pass the McDonald's. What do you know, there's a *horse*, a horse in Western tack standing in the drive-thru. I nearly override every instinct I possess and step down hard on the brakes. Fortunately, I regain my senses and slowly, slowly, come to a halt before the red light.

Where do I know that horse from? Finally, I register it's my oral surgeon, wearing a cowboy hat, on the palomino I saw in the waiting room photo.

"What are you doing?" I ask, rolling down the window and shouting at him across the road.

"I bet you couldn't take that English horse of yours to McDonald's like this," Dr. Roberts says, grinning, tipping his hat, and moseying off, holding a tiny white paper bag. He's in jeans and a short-sleeved plaid shirt.

The light changes. There's someone behind me, so I have to step on the gas.

When Sean and I were kids, sometimes we'd ride through the Wawa drive-thru. Sean would take his tank of a paint Camera Shy. Cam was one of those Western horses who could do a bit of everything—barrels, team penning, lower-level hunters. I even rode Cam in the jumpers once or twice. He'd never spook at anything. But my mare, Damsel, she'd shy and dance at the crackle of the loudspeaker.

The more popular he got in high school, the less my brother Sean rode. I'd exercise Cam on the trails. I'd stop at Wawa or McDonald's alone. People would honk horns and sometimes guys on bicycles would attempt to race us. Up in Vermont, it was quieter. Still, I had a run-in with a guy playing chicken on the road with my big grey horse, Fortune.

I arrive back at the barn, unload and hose the sticky dried foam off Morrissey. My shirt is heavy upon my skin. I can feel the sun burning through the fabric, blistering my back. After I've turned him out, I strip to the waist, rinse myself off with a spritz from the hose, towel myself off, spray sunscreen all over me, and throw on a sunshirt that's supposed to have SPF. With a baseball hat to top it all off, I feel like a new man, protected, professional, and ready for anything, and stride over to the main arena to teach my first lesson of the day. It's nine in the morning, which isn't that late, but already the horse that's hauled in is as sweaty as I was an hour ago after working.

"Don't expect too much of us today!" pleads Nancy. Her mare's energy wilts faster than her saddle pad. Nancy is a schoolteacher, a fact for which I've long forgiven her. She teaches math, a subject I like, and she approaches her riding with the same step-by-step precision of solving an equation. Although in math, I would always just kind of look at the problems and know the answer without scribbling much down, which usually earned me an accusation of cheating. As if I would bother to cheat at something as useless to me as school. It's why I'd be a terrible math teacher myself. Unlike my teacher-boyfriend, I have no patience when people can't calculate the answers I can see intuitively on a page.

The elements of riding I *have* learned to break down over the years. No matter how talented a rider is, there will always be a horse that defies his instincts. I've had to humble myself countless times, going back to basics like counting strides, remembering the power of the outside rein, and sitting rather than hovering light above the saddle.

Which is what I'm telling Nancy now. "Wait, wait, wait for it," I say, so she sits back and Luna takes off from the correct distance, not banging the top rail with her hooves. Luna is not the cattiest of horses, and she has a tendency of throwing herself at fences in careless, questionable ways. Horse and rider are a good match for one another, though, as Nancy likes to micromanage things. The last thing she'd want is a mount who demands you stay out of her way.

During a walk break, as we wait for Luna's breathing and brain to settle, I ask, "Have you ever taken Luna through a McDonald's drive-thru?"

"What kind of question is that? Are you proposing a field trip with Loony Luna?"

"Maybe. I saw my oral surgeon riding his horse through a drive-thru."

"I'm more of a Dunkin' woman myself."

"A rare show of good taste. As you know, Dunkin' is part of my culture, just like the Red Sox." I touch my lucky cap. Nancy roots for the Orioles. We've clashed about baseball many times before. Last lesson, I told her I'd make her wear my Red Sox cap if she didn't jump a clean course, so I could post the photo on Instagram. One of the rare bets I've lost.

She's not up for this one, though. "Thanks, but I'll stick to the car. I have enough problem reaching the window without opening up my door, much less navigating the drive-thru line on Luna."

I'm so excited about the idea of taking Morrissey on a road trip I call Eric on my way home. "You're going to do what?" asks Eric. It's hard to hear his voice over the air-conditioning and The Violent Femmes.

"I'm taking Morrissey through the drive-thru of the McDonald's tomorrow morning."

"In the trailer? Don't you do that already?"

"No! I mean riding him."

"Do you have a death wish?"

"About eating McDonald's or riding Morrissey?"

"You're going horseback riding on that busy road to the McDonald's?"

"You run on that busy road yourself. I've nearly run your sorry ass over."

"But my sorry ass doesn't belong to a flighty animal who spooks at flowers and ditches and things."

"Are we having dinner together? What should I pick up?"

"What if Morrissey gets hurt?" he asks. Then I feel warmly toward Eric. I've trained him well. He knows that the best way to get a horseman not to do something is to say it might be unsafe for his horse.

Over pepperoni pizza, I explain to Eric about how Morrissey is properly shod, and is used to cars and shouting from his racing days, as well as horse trials. I don't convince him, but I convince myself what I'm doing is a good idea, which more important. In fact, Eric's hesitancy only eggs me on to get my Egg McMuffin, because he's not a horse person. Usually, the opposite of a civilian's instinct is the right thing to do with horses. I'm still rankled by Callum's assertion that his calm horse, insensitive to the noise of fair-goers and parades, is better trained than mine. Plus Dr. Roberts's smile. I might not have time to become an expert at jousting right now, or rustling cows, but I can do this much.

Despite my bravado, I'm not entirely insane. I leave the house extra-early to take Morrissey schooling. I decide to walk back and forth to the McDonald's near the horse park, not the entire way from my barn.

There aren't many cars on the road this early. A bunch of lax bros in a Jeep, their lacrosse sticks hanging out of the backseat window, give me the finger. I wonder what they're doing since school is out. Then I remember Eric's at school, too. They're probably heading to practice, hungover from their late-night beer-and-Juul sucking fest. I still don't understand why the sight of a beautiful horse makes some people act so ugly. Still, I'm cautious enough to keep both hands on the reins and not give the lax bros the finger back. This is what you call wisdom, versus how wise-ass I was as a teen.

Morrissey makes a clip-clop on the pavement as close as you'll hear a horse sound like in the movies. His ears are up, which is unusual, and his head carriage is higher than normal. He arches his back, as if he's looking for a reason to spook, but can't quite find it. I lean down to give my order.

At the crackling sound of static, Morrissey shows off some Grand Prix dressage-worthy lateral work, though he's not at the "airs above ground" stage like Owen was at the horse park. I block him with the firm pressure of my leg so he doesn't go too far horizontally. He doesn't seem truly afraid of the talking box, though, more intrigued and unsure.

I have to lean down much farther than Dr. Roberts did to grab my white bag.

"I guess people come through the drive-thru on horses all the time?" I ask. I pay using my phone.

"No, just you and another guy," says the kid. He's got peeling acne crusting his face. I feel sorry for him. All the kids who worked fast food at my high school had terrible acne. The oil seeped into their pores. It looks even worse than what Sean calls my mick tan, my Irish-fair, freckled skin that peels under the blistering sun. When I was bored and couldn't get away with sleeping at my desk in high school, I'd pick at my freckled arms in class, stare out the window, and dream of horses. Leave a little pile of flaking white in protest on my chair in English class for the next kid.

I'm a little taken aback by how unimpressed the McDonald's guy is by my riding through the line, but he can't know Morrissey used to snap and shy if I curried the horse too vigorously or if the metal of the crossties rattled too hard. I dismount and walk my chestnut to the grass in front, rationalizing that if manure happens, it is serviceable fertilizer that the franchise owner would have to pay for otherwise.

I let my horse graze with the bridle as I eat and watch the cars whizz by. The sun is warm, and I'm already sweating, but the heat from the sun gives the biscuit sandwich some extra flavor, melting the nuclear cheesy filling a bit more before I shove it in my mouth, bite by bite.

"See, boy, I still know how to have fun on a horse," I say to Morrissey, a horse that's been nothing but work for me since the day I bought him. "Just like I was when I was a kid." I take another bit of grease-soaked biscuit. "I still know how to relax."

Back at the barn, I spy a message from Dr. Roberts on my phone.

I saw you eating at McDonald's. No sugar!

I fire off a response. *I got a sausage, egg, and cheese biscuit and a Coke. That's not much sugar.*

Since I'm texting a medical professional, I'm careful to punctuate. My lack of proper punctuation and capitalization when texting drove my first boyfriend Max crazy, which I always put down to his being much older than me. But I now acknowledge, grudgingly, it also bothers some of my clients, young and old.

I can't resist adding in one more bubble. *I saw you at McDonald's.*

Immediately, he texts back. *I get coffee there. No sugar. You call those eggs?*

I switch tactics. *You weren't wearing a helmet.*

He responds. *You're right. I'm old and stupid. At my age, I have nothing to prove.*

My phone springs to life with light and sound. Dr. Roberts! I'm slightly shocked, since every doctor I've ever encountered usually has several levels of office staff before speaking to me in person, like they're the Pope or something.

"I *own* a helmet."

"It's not doing you much good in your tack room. Trust me, my brother rode Western, often without a helmet unless required for a show, and he sucked. Not wearing a helmet doesn't make you an expert rider."

"You sound like my niece. *Put on a helmet, Uncle Russell. Just because you're riding Western doesn't mean you don't need a helmet, Uncle Russell.*"

"You're a dentist. Your brains are expensive. I protect mine, and they're not worth half so much, but definitely more than a McDonald's biscuit sandwich. Most days, anyway."

"Someday you need to come to my ranch and I'll give you Western lessons."

"You own a ranch?"

"Two Quarter Horses in a stable in my backyard, plus a couple of hound dogs and livestock. I also dabble in farming." I'm assuming it's a pretty nice backyard, given what oral surgeons make, especially the best oral surgeons in Baltimore County.

"You come to *my* farm, and I'll give you eventing lessons. I'll have you know I rode Western quite a lot as a kid and was pretty decent at barrel racing." I don't mention team penning. I never mention team penning. I owned a Thoroughbred who froze at the stink of cow.

During the week, I get a call from a Ms. Malloy, whose name means nothing to me until she introduces herself as Gretchen's mom of Rabbit Rabbit fame. "Gretchen is concerned Ainsley—who she loves, loves—doesn't quite understand Rabbit. We're looking for a new perspective." She's whispering so softly, I feel like I'm setting up a drug deal.

After the Malloy mom and kid trailer over for the lesson, I spend a long time warming up Gretchen, which seems to confuse the kid. We work on leg yields, shoulders in, haunches in. Gretchen shrugs when I ask if she understands what I'm making her do and why.

Next, I set up a gymnastic. The chute forces her to be more precise about the distances from which she jumps, more than my words. Not until the very end do I let Gretchen jump a full course. I require her to tell me how many strides she's going to ride to each jump, rather than simply turning and burning. Finally, she speaks, whispering (correctly) "five" or "four."

Gretchen's mother seems relieved her kid makes it through the lesson without generating an explosion of temper from me or an explosion of warp speed from the pony. The light-colored pony has darkened with sweat and his rider's face is pink.

"Once the jumps get bigger, if you're racing around like you were, you're more likely to pull a rail. I'm sure Ainsley told you that."

Gretchen nods.

Her mom says, "Gretchen wants to jump bigger, but Ainsley didn't think you were ready, right Gretchen?"

Gretchen shrugs.

Gretchen has unsaddled the pony. I guide her to the wash stall. Ms. Malloy explains they used to keep the pony at home, but moved to Fletch's now Gretchen wants to be more competitive. Gretchen sweat-scrapes the pony and leads Rabbit Rabbit onto the trailer. I don't think this kid has said a word to me the entire time she's been at the farm that I haven't pried out of her lips. It reminds me of how I was at that age. I feel this is a subtle kind of revenge by the universe upon me for my own behavior.

Dr. Roberts must be busy with work, because I don't spy the palomino at any drive-thrus for nearly a week. I do see Lena scooting around on her pink Vespa, though, with a pink motorcycle helmet to match.

"Nice to see that someone in your family protects their brain," I call to her from my car, opening the window and slowing down. "Your uncle inspired me to take Morrissey through the drive-thru at McDonald's. Just like I saw him do with his horses."

"Simon! My uncle's horses are as pretty close to bombproof as you can get. Morrissey at a drive-thru? You crazy?" She revs the cheerfully sputtering little engine.

We both know the answer to that question. "I lived! Besides, there's no such thing as a totally broke horse, we both know that. Now you need to try Owen at a Beginner Novice event!"

I expect her to say something funny back, but she just shrugs. It's hard to tell beneath the helmet, but I could swear she's in a funk. "Are you doing anything particular for lunch? I promise not to take you to McDonald's."

"Let's go to Auntie's."

Auntie's is an upscale soul food brunch chain that's just taken off. The one we go to is near a boutique strip mall near a very chic tack store that caters to the matchy-matchy hunter-jumper crew, a custom cabinet store, and a Princeton Review. Lena says she goes for private tutoring for the SAT math section.

"I did really well on my PSATs. Not to brag, just an observation, because I never used the scholarship I won," I say.

"I wish you'd offer to tutor me in math, rather than keep pushing your horse on me."

"Not a chance."

"I applied to a few jumper barns as a groom. And as an assistant trainer to another, for a barn I thought I was overqualified."

"I knew it! There's no help for you, Lena." She's just as addicted as I am.

"None of them called me back."

The waitress comes to take our order. I contemplate how to admit I eavesdropped on her conversation with Ainsley. Finally, I just say it flat out. "You know how you thought I was all doped up after my surgery? Well, I wasn't, and heard about all your grief with Paula."

"I'll have the cornbread with extra honey butter, and a side of turkey bacon," she says to the waitress. She turns back to me. "You might have let us know."

"No eggs with your bacon?" I ask her.

"I hate eggs."

"Who hates eggs?"

"They smell weird to me."

I order ham and sweet potato waffles. "Agreed. I should have said something. But everyone in this industry has a Paula story, or has heard enough about her to run the other way. A barn that would take her word rather than yours isn't worth worrying about."

"I'm sick of always wondering if people are only treating me badly and judging me just because that's how the horse world is, or if it's because of who I am. If I get disrespected and I know something's not right, people always say stuff like, 'Well, that's just Paula.' I'll never know if she treated me slightly worse or much worse than her other working students and clients."

"Let it go, Lena. You learned an important lesson. In the horse world, you always have to put yourself first. Never confuse your own interests with your employer's interests. Every horseperson has a magic box of smoke and mirrors to confuse you that they are the same. Don't let them fool you."

The waitress serves Lena's order before mine. There's a wait on the ham.

"It's easy to say 'let it go,' when you're not mistaken for the groom at every show." Lena vigorously butters a slice of cornbread. "I mean, I have done a groom's work, but I've spent my whole life trying to be a better rider."

"There's no shame in being a groom," I say.

"Never said there was. I just want respect as a rider, too." She pokes at the crumbs that have fallen from the slice before taking a bite of bread.

"You know I respect you," I say. But then I feel guilty. I can't pretend I haven't looked the other way more than a few times when people have said things in my career as a horseman. Sometimes there's just so much shit to deal with. So I don't speak up when a new farrier—who knows how to shoe a Thoroughbred's finicky soft soles just right—starts spouting off on his crazy-ass political views. I don't agree with him, of course. But I don't confront him. Is that just as bad?

Hell, I probably have made some jokes I shouldn't have, like in high school when I used to joke about how I was the only white kid in my AP math classes. The barns I rode at were all white, and there was no one around to tell me what I said was wrong. People were saying far worse, until I started dating my first boyfriend, who was older than me, and knew there was more to measuring a person's character than how well he could stick on a horse.

There's a lot of ugly noise in the horse world. Eventually you just tune it out and become numb to it, just like how I dealt with the country music that blasted on the barn radios when I couldn't control the playlist as a teen. That numbness is my luxury, not Lena's. It's easier to be numb, to ignore things.

I've vowed not to do it when it comes to the welfare of my horses, but sometimes human welfare gets shoved to the side. Ignoring what's in front of you can kill you on a horse, and perhaps ignoring what I've sometimes ignored is just as killing in its own way to a person's soul. My own, as well as the souls of others.

"Paula's still in my head, telling me I'm not good enough. My uncle said, always keep a little bit of yourself for yourself. I'm not sure that's possible as a horse pro. For me."

I can't say that's not true, because I certainly haven't. I have given up everything for horses, not just sweat, but my own sense of fairness and justice and sanity and quality of life. When someone can shoe a horse, ride, or train a horse correctly, even beautifully, I look the other way at everything else, assuming someone can't be all bad, if that person is good with horses. I have even given up a man's love for horses, the way I needled and picked at Phillip when he was winning on Morrissey and I was not.

"I can't not be emotionally invested in the horses that I ride. It's like, when I first started riding Pilot after we retired Leo, everyone was impressed I could get winning rides out of him. I was a junior, and his past rider, a really strong guy, wasn't getting him to behave. But *I could ride a horse no one else could ride and win on him.* Like a horse girl in a movie. It made me feel so good, especially because we were only able to buy him cheaply because of his reputation. Then, he started to misbehave, even with me. Even with Vince, when I put him into boot camp. The vet couldn't find anything. It was all in his head. I felt like I failed him, as well as myself."

"Hey, he's the one who dumped you in a pile of poles," I say, feeling on surer ground with the Pilot issue. "There are always some horses that get the better of you. You can't make a horse love the life. Competition. Pressure. Adrenaline. Just like humans, there are some athletic and talented horses that would rather be pasture puffs or lower-level dressage horses. That's not a reason to blame yourself and quit riding."

I want to make, well, everything up to Lena. Everything I've done wrong over the years, and I don't just mean putting her on Owen that day to avenge myself against Phillip. I realize I can't. Some things can't be forgiven. I just have to live with my own guilt about what I've said, done, and not done. That's on me, not on her, and I have no business asking for any kind of forgiveness I don't deserve.

"When I posted on Instagram about Pilot's accident, Paula commented, *He got rid of some heavy baggage.* I forgot I hadn't blocked her on that account. I knew what she must be saying behind my back. That little comment of hers got I don't know how many hearts until I deleted the whole post."

"Let it go, Lena. It's one thing if you want to leave the horse world for you. It's another thing to be bullied out of it."

"You're trying to bully me into trying your crazy-ass eventing." Delicately, she butters another golden, crumbling slice.

"Beginner Novice-level eventing is a walk-trot test, and fences are itty-bitty. In fact, you get penalties if you go too fast, not just too slow at that level. You'll feel like you're back on ponies."

"Simon, stop trying to convert me! You should have pamphlets or something, like the Witnesses, to stick in people's mailboxes. Owen is no pony."

My ham and waffles have finally arrived. They're heart-shaped and powdered with sugar, which makes me leery. "Don't eat it right away, it's extremely hot," warns the waitress. Still, I'm hungry, so I immediately spear the center, saw of a bit of the crackling brown-orange heart, as well as some pork, and shove a forkful of steaming ham and powdered waffle in my mouth. Eric had to work late. I was too cranky and suspicious to have a real dinner by myself, opting for nothing but a bowl of cereal and bile to nurse over the gay fantasy werewolf book I downloaded on my phone to keep my brain occupied.

"Ow!" I mutter. I think I lost the first layer of skin inside my mouth right there.

"I'm trusting your good judgement," says Lena.

"At least I can chew solid foods again." I keep shoveling food in my face, slathering the waffle with cinnamon-infused butter and cooling it with the smoky maple syrup on the table rather than waiting. "My treat, by the way."

"They won't charge us. My Aunt Cici owns the chain."

"No way!"

"My aunt was named one of the top up-and-coming Black woman restauranteurs by Eater last month," brags Lena.

"Is everyone in your family outrageously successful and famous or what?"

"Some of them are too successful."

"How is it possible to be too successful?"

"Like my cousin Michelle. She's a YouTuber."

"A what?"

"Like, she makes videos for YouTube, tutorials, posts them, and monetizes them."

"So?"

"Uncle Russell is beside himself. You think he's passionate about flossing, you should see him about going to college. She wants to quit school and do it full-time."

"She makes enough money doing that? Like, what kind of videos? School stuff? Bad stuff?"

"No, no, no! Makeup tutorials. Like how to give yourself cat's eyelids with liquid liner, contouring, that sort of thing. Haven't you heard of the channel Black Girl Beauty Magic?"

"I hope I don't totally destroy my cred as a gay man when I say I haven't."

"She's working with a company and developed her own line of skin and hair care products. She thinks she can become an influencer, her own brand for a living. She doesn't want to go to college anymore. She used to want to go to Emory."

"No Harvard?"

"Too cold. She went to some national science fair thing up there and it took her a week to recover. She's delicate. Emory is the Harvard of the South."

"Your uncle will save a lot of money. No student loans for her."

"It's all everyone talks about in the family! I suppose I should be grateful they aren't talking about me and my cracked femoral neck and Pilot anymore."

"How is what she doing so terrible? Here I am, training horses in the pissing rain and boiling heat, day in and day out, like a sucker, and your cousin hasn't even graduated from high school and is making a living putting on makeup in front of a camera in her bedroom. I'm lucky if I can get a sponsor to give me a pair of free breeches to put on my sorry bare ass."

"A lot more people wear makeup than ride, Simon."

"So I'm finding out!" I spear the perfect ratio of waffle, butter, and ham onto my fork. This is possibly the best waffle I've ever consumed, even if it is in the shape of a heart. I'm increasingly in awe of Lena's family members and their many gifts.

"My uncle planned on Michelle majoring in chemistry and working for a pharmaceutical company or something like that. Once she hit the one million subscriber threshold, her AP science grades went way down. You can tell he's mad at her by his Facebook posts. He's stopped posting photos about how proud he is of his baby, and instead just posts blurry pictures of his horses, dogs, chickens, and cherry tomatoes from his garden. Look." She whips out her phone to show me.

"When your children disappoint you, there's always the comfort of growing a tomato, I guess. I speak as someone who has been letting my family down for two decades plus." Mom wanted to me to work for a cushy (and safe) hunter show barn. Kind of like what Ainsley is doing right now. My physics teacher, who was a really nice guy, wanted me to apply to college and study engineering.

"My uncle really likes you, by the by. You're on the waiting list for the next family reunion."

"The what?"

"My family has a reunion every five years. We rent out several rooms of a hotel. It's a big deal. There's a waiting list, though."

"Sounds like a lot of pressure. My family keeps holidays low-key by alienating most of our relatives, and usually most of the people we've been dating by Thanksgiving every year.

I think we're just doing ours in a restaurant, come November."

"A restaurant for Thanksgiving! I'm shook. Do you think you're going to alienate Eric by fall?"

I pause in my hoovering. "No. No, I don't think so. I hope not. Anyway, I won't be offended if I don't make the reunion cut, before the boyfriends and girlfriends of your blood kin."

"Oh, you wouldn't necessarily be lower on the list than some of them. My Aunt Cici's boyfriend tried to take over the grill and smoker last Memorial Day from Uncle Russell, and it got ugly. He even criticized my uncle's famous homemade barbeque sauce."

"Let me guess, not enough sugar in it?"

"It was a scene. When my uncle puts on his apron, you stand back and accept your plate, you do not critique your food. Still, you're right, there can be a lot of pressure to do something extraordinary in my family."

"Your family reunion sounds like a club with a very aggressive bouncer. Even some of the gay clubs I've gone to haven't had that high a standard."

"If you come, you definitely need to upgrade your footwear," she says, looking at my battered barn Doc Martens (which is admittedly a step down from my usual going-out Docs).

Chapter 6

Hot For Teacher

Eric is on my couch with his laptop open on his stomach. I know he's looking over his student's essays. I should leave him alone. This is his work; he respects my time working with horses, even though he doesn't understand them.

I can't help it. His seriousness is like a scab I must scratch and pick. Memories of how much I hated school come flooding back. I lean over, blow on his glasses to fog them.

"Stop that!" he says. He grins at me, cleans the lenses on his shirt, but his eyes shift back to the screen. Away from me.

"I never knew I wouldn't be able to have sex with a teacher whenever I wanted during the summer," I pout, pushing my body snugly beside him and draping my arm over his shoulder.

"You'll have to wait for the school supplies to be on sale for anything really kinky," he murmurs.

"A nice, sturdy pencil gripper? For sinister lefties like myself? Speaking of trying new things, Lena's going eventing." At least that should get his attention.

"Simon, why won't you leave that poor woman alone? I thought you said she wants to get out of horses." I watch him raise a hand to insert a little bubble of a comment. He does so without missing a beat of the conversation or breaking eye contact with the screen.

"Because Lena's doing the dance, the same dance all horsey folk do. Vows to get out of horses, then gets back into horses." It's a bizarre hokey-pokey. Like some bands with a never-ending series of farewell tours.

"I guess I shouldn't even pretend to understand."

"Eric, I don't mean to pry. But why won't you give riding another chance? You haven't been on a horse since you were, what, sixteen?"

"Why is it so important to you I ride?" he asks, eyes fixated upon his laptop, avoiding my prying gaze. His mood has suddenly shifted. He looks genuinely afraid, and I don't think it's of his students' grammar.

"Because horses are my life, and I want you to be a bigger part of my life, and not afraid," I say, trying to push myself into him. This is the most intimate thing I've said to a man since Phillip. Towards the end, things were so bad I never thought or said *I love you*. Phillip and I could only make up through sex in the dark, not talking in the light of day.

"I've helped you out at your horse shows. Didn't you break up with your ex because of an argument about a horse? Why do you need me to ride?" Eric asks.

"We won't break up because of riding, Eric."

"Because you know I won't be any good at it, unlike your ex."

I touch my lips to his neck. I'm lanky and thin, and Eric's a smaller person, lean and muscular from all his running, but it's still a tight squeeze on my couch. I grab his ear with my teeth. It's an outlet for the little bubble of rage I feel. How does he know me too well?

"Drama and music are a part of who I am. You never come to see the plays I direct. Stop biting my ear so I can finish grading and kiss you back."

"But you're just the director. They're high school plays with high school kids. I don't care about a play if you're not in it."

He sighs. He's annoyed. This turns me on, so I keep poking and nibbling at him, trying not to slide off onto the carpet. God knows what's down there. You could eat off the floors of my horse's stalls, but don't look down in my house.

"I mean, all you do is grade papers and help your kids do theater and forensics."

"All you do is ride and teach. If I rode, it would be for you and only for you. I wouldn't enjoy it."

"How do you know?"

"Because I ended up on the ground last time I climbed on the back of a horse?"

"You should do something that scares you every day."

"But nothing scares you, and everything scares me," he said, ferociously typing a comment in a little bubble. "So that doesn't really work, does it?"

"You can't live in fear."

"Yet I'm still alive."

I kiss him. He kisses back, then it's back to the laptop.

"Fine, fuck you," I say.

"Not everyone is like you."

"What's that supposed to mean?"

"Successful."

"I'm not successful."

"The fact you're so careless about your own success is incredibly annoying, Simon."

"I mean, I'm not as successful as I'd like."

"Boo-hoo."

"I'm afraid of the dentist." He shrugs. Now I'm mad. I've never admitted I'm afraid of something to anyone so boldly. "You're a successful teacher. You run your class with an iron fist."

"In a velvet glove. How very medieval of me. Or Renaissance. I know how you feel about that."

"You impressed me when I came to visit you at school."

"I wish my students felt the same way."

"Who is this Dylan Clarke guy?"

Eric closes the document, shuts down the computer with a sigh, then closes the plastic black PC shell itself. I know it's normal to save all the hard work he's done, and it's a kid's private essay he's protecting. But the fussiness of his care about something that's not a living creature, that's just words on a screen, seems like a sign he doesn't want me. I hear a click in my ear as I grind my teeth hard.

"You've been scrolling through my phone without my permission?"

"When I was holding it for you at the Faire." I hesitate before saying, "and when I saw it light up lying around my house one day."

Eric gets pissed. Quietly. Like a teacher gets pissed. He climbs over me, although I try to block him with my body on the couch. I'm surprised by how agile he can be when he has a goal in mind.

"I need to make a call," he says.

He picks up his cell, but rather than slinking into another room, he puts the phone on speaker. A voice fills the room. A voice radiating from the ripped abs of a guy who can't *not* speak from his diaphragm, I'm guessing. "What's doing, Eric?"

"My boyfriend Simon is looking to take singing lessons from you, Dylan," he says.

"What is he? Tenor? Baritone? Base?" Dylan doesn't miss a beat, like this is a normal thing to ask.

"I don't know. What are you, Simon?"

"I'm thinking," I say.

"Let me check my book. Would right after your usual slot work?" says Dylan.

"I'll ask him, thanks." Eric hangs up. "Simon, I've been taking singing lessons. Show tune singing lessons. So jazzy. So gay."

"Fuck you, Eric, you know I don't think that way. You're the one who was skulking around, hiding our relationship from work for ages."

"I work at a Catholic school!"

"I think it's great you're taking singing lessons!" I'm shouting at him. "Now maybe you'll get off the couch and start auditioning again."

"I work a full-time teaching job, plus run several extracurriculars, Simon. Just because I'm not always at a barn 24/7 doesn't mean I don't work."

"I didn't say that."

"I'm not going back to auditioning. This is for me! I'm taking lessons because I love singing. To relax!" He's almost shouting. Again, he gets mad just like a teacher.

"I can fucking tell it's working!" Real shouting, to relieve the tension.

"I don't want casting directors to judge me ever again." He picks up his laptop and starts putting on his shoes.

"Christ on cracker, don't flounce the fuck off like that," I say. He's disgusted with me. I'm disgusted with myself. I've checked his phone, invaded his privacy, assumed the worst, and accused him of not doing a decent day's work as a teacher, because it's not his passion.

I don't need this stress. I have a complicated horse in my life. I don't need a complicated man, a man with all these insecurities about his own worth. I'm better off with fuck boys like Phillip, who just drift and take for granted they are worthy of love. I care too much about Eric, even though he doesn't care much for himself, and that scares me worse than the dentist.

I stand in front of Eric, take him in my arms, and kiss him. His tongue and his skin are warm against mine. "I'm sorry," I say. God, I hate this strange man for making me frightened he might leave me.

Naked, we watch an episode of Doctor Who after our fight and share a bag of potato chips and soda for dinner. Eric's favorite television show is growing on me. If I can learn to love a British kid's science fiction show, surely he can come and sit on one of my horses. Isn't that love? Isn't that compromise? I check my texts.

"Christ on a cracker," I say, for the second time this evening.

"Are the horses okay?"

"Nancy fell off schooling Luna tonight and dislocated a shoulder, so she won't be able to lesson tomorrow," I mutter. "Other than that, everything's fine." She must have gone over late to beat the heat and got beat up by the ground instead.

"I'm so sorry," he says.

"It happens." Now I'll have to ride lazy Luna, get up even earlier, since the horse doesn't do well in the humidity. Luna will be my leg workout for the day.

"You're not really selling me on the horseback riding thing."

"When I dislocated my shoulder, I just popped it back in and got back on. But Nancy is more delicate."

"Still not selling it."

"True, selling horses has never been one of my greatest talents. Otherwise, Owen would have been long gone by now."

"If you press me, I'll make you take a singing lesson for reals," Eric says. I run my fingers through his hair, and I admit I shudder a bit at the idea of anyone listening to me sing anywhere but the shower. I love music; I have enough

112

of an ear to carry a tune and to know my singing voice is not my gift.

Still, it's hard for me to, I don't know, really empathize with someone who is afraid of horses. I feel like there must be something lacking in someone who doesn't ride, like there's a gaping wound in Eric that he won't let me heal.

Slowly, I have learned to have compassion for people who have developed rational fears of certain aspects of riding. Eric only cares for horses as much as they concern me, and in the sense that he would never be deliberately cruel to another living creature. If I gave horses up tomorrow, he'd never think about riding. It's baffling.

My phone rings again. "Nancy?" I ask.

"This is Serena St. Claire."

"Oh my God!" says Eric. He stands up, like it's the Queen of fucking England. By this time, I figure Ms. St. Claire and I are on sitting terms, although I wrap my blanket around myself, concealing my nakedness though she can't see me.

"A pleasure to speak with you again," I say, and, mainly because I'm sure she heard Eric in the background, "my friend is a big fan of yours." He puts his head in his hands, as if groveling in respect and humiliation. Thank God, Buddha, Brandon Flowers of The Killers, or whatever deity you worship, this isn't a Facetime call.

"I understand you've encouraged my daughter to enter, a what do you call it, a horse trial?"

Just the way she says *trial* makes me feel like I've done something illegal. "A little one-day show. With tiny, tiny fences." I say *show*, because it sounds harmless. Like showbiz. Or show tunes. Now I'm the one desperately waving jazz hands to distract her.

I put the phone on speaker and sit down. I may be naked, but I'm assuming a power position, feet planted, seat bones balanced. Also, I want a witness to the conversation in case I go missing in the near future.

Eric walks over to where I left the stuffed beaver I won hatchet-throwing at the Renaissance Faire, picks it up, and cradles it in his arms, hugging it close, to deal with his pent-up, fidgety energy. We still haven't named Mr. Beaver.

"Mr. O' Shaughnessy, I happen to know eventing is one of the most dangerous things you can do with a horse on this planet," says Serena.

Eric mouths *holy shit* at me. The stuffed animal's eyes stare at me, beady and angry.

"Your daughter is a very capable rider, Ms. St. Claire. It's true that riding cross-country has more risks than riding in an arena, given the footing and—"

"Jumps that don't fall down," says Serena.

Why is this the one thing everyone knows about eventing, even non-horsey people?

"I can't even watch my daughter jump fences in an arena without covering my eyes."

Speaking with Ms. St. Claire is indeed a historic experience for me. Not because of her fame, for I have dealt with rich and famous people before. But because I realize I have just encountered someone with as sensitive a bullshit detector as my own. The dog-and-pony show I usually put on about helmets and inflatable vests meets a brick wall in the person of Serena St. Claire. She knows horseback riding, especially the jumping disciplines, can be dangerous. She knows *I know* horseback riding is dangerous. The risk is worth it to me. It's not worth it to her, concerning her daughter.

"I've been talking to my brother *the cowboy*. Even he says eventing is risky."

"Your brother doesn't wear a helmet all the time! All of my riders wear helmets, every minute they're on a horse." I don't mention the reason I have this rule is that I got a concussion from not wearing a helmet when I was young, teenaged, and dumb, and can't afford another. One more strike, and I'm out.

"Risk is everywhere," I say, gesturing wildly with my hands.

"Horses are unpredictable animals. Everything is more dangerous when horses are in the picture."

But also more fun. "Dr. Roberts rides his horse to McDonald's."

"My brother is a *fool*. He's an oral surgeon. He keeps two horses in his suburban backyard—outdated zoning laws, you know—and suddenly, he's a cowboy."

"He owns a couple of hounds."

"Two miniature long-haired dachshunds! Named Beverly and Wyatt."

"He said he had livestock?"

"Two chickens, Bernice and Thelma! Which he keeps in this little Victorian structure. It's ridiculous, the coup looks like a house! Nicer than some of the houses I've lived in! Except when I was over one Thanksgiving, he kept them in the laundry room, on a heating pad, because it was too cold. Do you know what chickens smell like, Mr. Simon O' Shaughnessy?"

Maybe this is the source of Lena's inexplicable hatred of eating eggs. "I know what chicken nuggets smell like."

"I mean, chickens not on your plate! Live chickens do not smell pleasant!"

"Doesn't he farm?"

"Heritage tomato plants! Every time a tomato ripens or one of those horrible chickens lays an egg, I get a text message or hear about it on Facebook."

"Oh." I run my tongue over my no-longer-constantly-sore gums. "Well, I appreciate his talent as an oral surgeon."

"Enough about my brother. My daughter is a grown woman, of course, and I suppose she'll make her own mistakes." I have a feeling riding with me is one of those mistakes. "But please try to keep her in one piece." She hangs up.

Eric is still staring, open-mouthed. He puts down the beaver.

"That was amazing," he says.

"Better than Broadway?" I ask. "Hopefully Lena won't dislocate her shoulder like Nancy. Her mother will pull both of my arms out of their sockets, and then go back to memorizing her lines on her treadmill, without a beat."

The phone rings again. "Christ on a cracker, time to throw this thing in a bucket of water."

It's Ainsley Ashcroft. Not funny, gossipy Ainsley Ashcroft, but Ainsley Ashcroft, assistant to the respected hunter trainer Fletcher Cox. "Simon O' Shaughnessy, I thought we were friends!"

We were?

"You poached my student!"

"I what? Poached?" My mind is still in egg mode.

"Gretchen Malloy? Rabbit Rabbit? What gives?"

"Ainsley, it's late, I'm enjoying, or, rather, was trying to enjoy a quiet night with my boyfriend, watching a rerun episode starring the Tenth Doctor Who. One of the hotter Doctors. I gave Gretchen Malloy a lesson. I'm confused what you mean by poaching."

"You don't steal people's students."

"Ainsley, let me explain, since your brain is back in hunter mode. If you remember correctly, in the eventing world, riders don't just have one trainer. I have a dressage trainer, a showjumping trainer, and I've taken clinics with a bunch of upper-level riders. You don't own this kid's horse, and you don't own the kid's business. It's the Malloy's pony, they can take lessons with whomever they want." I look over at Eric, to see if he's impressed by my *whom*.

"Not at my barn, they can't!"

She means Fletch's barn. God, I hate the attitude of some hunter trainers. "How did Gretchen do during her last show?"

"That's not the point."

"I can look up the results on my phone."

"Okay, she won! But you still poached her from me! I have my eye on you. You're on my stank list!"

She hangs up.

I turn to Eric. "Do you want to make love to a wanted man? My days on this earth are clearly numbered."

"I'll risk it."

"You're braver than you make yourself out to be," I say, and put the phone as far away from us as possible. I don't turn it off, though. It's the witching hour, but that doesn't stop horses from being horses. It's only a matter of time before one of them gets injured, or injures me.

Chapter 7
Practice Losing Faster

The team of O' Shaughnessy Eventing arrives at the horse trial venue later than expected, despite allowing plenty of time for the commute and any difficulties with Owen loading. It's bumper-to-bumper traffic, not because of our event, but for—you guessed it—some other Faire or festival going on nearby. I can even see the rigged-up spinning swing ride in the distance.

It's the sort of ride I always used to beg for multiple turns on until I could hardly walk straight. *Ha!* One fair, when I was still a little skinny kid, I actually got banned from all the rides. I tried to slide through the safety bar and stand up on the seat on one of them. Now I've matured regarding my respect for safety devices. That swing ride was pretty lame, anyway.

Today's trial is a small horse trial. Once we get to the actual park, the trailers and cars are spaced far apart. Lena and my student Rose are the sole students competing under my watch. Rose usually trailers over to my place from the dressage barn where she boards. She's an eventer, but the private, low-key barn filled mostly with ladies schooling second level or below is cheaper than mine and closer to her house. She only recently qualified for the Preliminary level in eventing.

On the way over, sweating the unexpected traffic, I explain to Lena, everyone in eventing has definite ride times, so if we get there late, she's got to be mentally prepared to go in cold. "I'm used to it," she says, grimly. "When I saw that my first dressage test was at 8:27 AM, I got confused," she admits. In the hunter-jumper world she comes from, it's not unusual for people to have their times jiggled around so their trainers can watch them or because people are constantly adding and scratching classes. In eventing, getting everyone through all three phases is enough of an organizational challenge. The organizers will grant me no special favors, despite my reputation.

Eric follows our horse trailer in his car. Rose will meet us there. He's here to wipe boots, hold horses, and do all the unenviable things that need doing that require little-to-no horse knowledge. He's bringing his car because it's always good to have an extra vehicle around in case we forget something. Or need to speed to Urgent Care ASAP.

"Make good choices," I say to Lena, giving her a leg up. "Remember, if you get hurt—your mom will hurt me worse. My ass is on the line," I say.

"I can't believe my mother called you. I'm so ashamed," says Lena. "I feel like I'm back in high school."

"Don't be. I'm used to it. You should see my mom if one of her students chips a fence." I try to sound casual, but I admit, I'm hoping Lena gets through this in one piece, because I know I will have to answer to a higher authority, fairly or unfairly. By higher authority, I mean Serena St. Claire, not God, and in a way, I'd prefer the latter, because God occasionally shows some mercy.

The cold black cavern in my chest I sometimes call a heart goes out to the teen riding a test right before Lena, on a jigging, prancing Thoroughbred.

"Been there," I say to the rider as she exits the sandbox. She is stone-faced, biting her lip in anger more than fear, mute in the face of my sympathy.

Lena's Beginner Novice test is, well, it is what it is. Seemingly endless trotting, even though the actual test only lasts for a few minutes. It's uneventful, which is what I guess you want lower-level eventing dressage to be. Since I had to get up so early and chastely limited myself to a single Coke, I'm too tired to say much. I am proud of what a good boy Owen is, though.

"Didn't Phillip Stone used to ride that horse? Looks familiar," I hear. I turn and see two sturdy-looking blonde girls watching from the rail, in the unofficial between-round eventer's uniform of sunshirts, baseball caps, and Boggs boots.

"I think his grey was darker." Greys fade with age, so this overheard conversation is a reminder of how long ago Phillip rode Owen regularly, before he took on Morrissey, then took off and out of my life entirely.

"Whatever happened to Phillip? He was so good on that horse."

I leave before I hear the answer. Sometimes I feel, much like dressage, I don't even understand what happened to Phillip. Though I should be an expert on men who leave by now.

Lena and I locate Rose and Eric. Rose has parked her trailer next to mine. I'm a little embarrassed to say this about one of my adult riders, but Rose is a grown-ass woman who rides a pony, a little stocky draft named Finnegan. He's a Welsh Cob, with some Quarter Horse and maybe some Morgan thrown into the pony genetic blender for good measure. *Closer to the ground, closer to hell*, I've always said about ponies. Being a Thoroughbred person is part of my self-image as both a rider and a trainer.

Rose is short and slight. Kitted out in her white breeches, stock tie, deep blue dressage coat, and matching navy helmet, she looks almost like a kid playing dress-up on Finnegan. Like me, she has fair, freckled skin. The freckles make her look old and young all at once, though she's redheaded rather than dirty blond, like me. Eric's wiping off her boots. I'd joke I've trained him well, but it's not all due to me, really. There's something in Eric's theater background that snaps into high gear when he hears "showtime." Even with horses.

"Remind me before they ring the bell to give you my whip," Rose pleads. "I know I'm going to need it." The trick with Finnegan is getting him in front of the rider's leg.

There's a crush of riders in the small, official warmup ring. We decide to school right outside it, not because we're worried about Finnegan being spooky or explosive, but it's hard to get a lazy horse forward in a small ring filled with other riders. That's why Rose has her sparkly whip in hand, which she affectionately calls her magic stick. She doesn't use it very much, but its presence acts as a warning to Finnegan to use himself back to front.

Fortunately, Finnegan, who is usually completely unimpressed by the O' Shaughnessy Eventing dressage ring, seems more alert in the entirely new surroundings. His ears are forward and he actually has some energy in his walk and trot. Then, suddenly, he springs forth into a canter of ground-covering power. My stream of words, of "seat" and "don't saw with your hands," and, "shorten your reins" slowly trails off into silence. Finnegan has more energy, and Rose doesn't have to work as hard as she usually does, so the pair creates an effortlessly pretty picture.

"I think he saw something that surprised him. I tried to use that energy for pony good, not pony evil," says Rose.

I look over my shoulder to see what Finnegan may have spied.

No.

No.

No.

It's Callum Rudd and his friend. Callum is wearing a billowing black cape, over-the-knee leather boots, and he's holding a sword. Isn't there another Faire going on around here? Why isn't he there? He claimed not to even know what eventing was. He doesn't even have his horses with him.

"Earth to Simon?" asks Rose. "My test is soon."

Guess I'll have to multitask my multiple crises. I watch my rider enter the official warmup ring. Take things test by test. I'll figure out what to do about Lena later.

Callum waves at me. Like we're buddies. "Ah, this is eventing. The organizers invited Sam and me to do a broadsword demonstration. Then we're heading over to another Faire."

Faire-fucking-tastic. Vaguely, I understand, with the functioning part of my brain that's not given over to rage, why they're here. It's hard enough to get volunteers and vendors at these types of schooling shows, so they've brought in this little sideshow, along with a few saddle and boot venders.

"Could you broadsword more quietly? You're right near the warmup area."

"Simon, please. I don't mind," says Rose. She's more afraid of my temper than of Callum's antics.

"It's okay, we're not scaring the little pony," he says, grinning.

Little pony? Finnegan is, well, cute. But he's taken Rose up to Preliminary, which is no minor feat.

After we're out of earshot, I hiss, "It's not Finnegan I'm worried about, it's Lena. It's her first horse trial."

"Lena doesn't seem nervous. She's a much more experienced rider than me, even though this is her first time eventing!"

"She hides her nerves well." Too well. I stand by the fence, and the bell sounds, heralding the start of Rose's test.

Rose's Preliminary-level dressage test has leg yields, and I involuntarily, half-subconsciously, bend my own body as

Rose tries to coax chunky Finnegan into something that resembles lateral, bending motion. The test is super-solid—not spectacular, but there are no errors. I can still hear the yelling and sword-clinking. I wonder if I'm crazy and have become overly sensitive until the woman at my left looks at me and shakes her head. "Why did they do this to the riders?"

Callum and his friend are not quite loud enough for me to feel justified complaining, but loud enough so I see dead calm Finnegan flick a cold-blooded, pale palomino ear now and then and transition a beat or two too late because he's distracted.

When we untack the pony, there's a dark chestnut splotch against his coat where his pad was, and sweat soaking his chest. "Good job," I say to Rose, who is looking pretty overheated and pink herself. "In fact, great job, under the circumstances." Circumstances meaning dressage in the heat on a pony whose ancestors roamed the damp, foggy cloudy hills.

Eric brings a bucket and sponge, and tentatively holds onto the lead rope as he sponges water on Finnegan. At my barn, he actively avoids getting close to the horses, but when I need him, he'll push through his fear.

I tap Lena on the shoulder. "Do you have a moment?" She's already in her navy showjumping coat and white breeches. A weird bubble of laughter creeps up my throat. "Our friends are here."

"Friends?"

"The LARP-ers. They're doing some kind of swordplay demonstration, for everyone's entertainment."

"No! I'm cursed! Entertainment? The entertainment's going to be seeing me launched off of Owen," she says.

I open my mouth, then shut it. I've read enough on the Internet about talking through a rider's fear or anxiety. I guess I should say things about visualization and breathing. But I've always felt like a liar when I speak about that woo-woo stuff, because I never do those things themselves. I mean, I breathe, but when I compete, I'm in a mental tunnel. I'm aware of everything around me, yet focused on nothing else, not the past or the future. Any attempt to divert my attention or energy means nothing. I don't need to meditate or check my horoscope or do any of that bullshit.

"Lena, sometimes the more you focus on making something not happen, the more likely it's going to happen. Try to think positively. Or we can go home. It's up to you."

"I want to do this," she says, slowly.

"Good! I know you want to do this! You may just have to focus a little harder to make it happen."

The stadium phase comes next. It used to be in eventing the showjumping always came last, but at smaller events like this, showjumping can often reverse in order with the cross-country portion, to accommodate the riders' schedules at different levels and if they're riding multiple horses. The horse gods are with us, and when Lena and Owen are in the arena, there's dead silence. Callum is practicing elsewhere.

Watching Lena, I can appreciate the essence of showjumping—it's not the height that matters, but the technique. These jumps are far, far lower than anything she's ridden in competition lately. But she doesn't hit a sloppy distance the entire round. She doesn't need to go for speed, only to jump clear. Every turn is tidy, and economical. There's quiet applause when she completes the course.

"Is that the showjumper Lena Roberts? I didn't know she evented," I hear blonde ponytail No. 2 say from the sidelines, the one who was wondering where Phillip was.

"I think so. My grandma watches her mom on TV all the time."

Rose pulls three rails, which is about par for the course with her lazy, sloppy pony. I'm not happy, but at least it's no worse than she's done at the level below. Rose, Lena, and the horses head back to our trailers to rest before the cross-country phase. Again, I hear the clank of swords. Owen spooks, rolls his eyes, and stiffens. Lena gives him a firm pat, but frowns.

"Once again, I'm asking, would you mind not doing that so near the horses? The riders have enough to deal with," I say.

"The organizers said we could practice wherever we wanted," says Callum.

"I understand, but you need to be respectful. Do you need to do this right under a horse's left nostril?"

"Hey, a car once backfired near Bailey during a joust, and he didn't care," says Callum.

"Great. I've ridden with cars going off and low-flying planes overhead. Shit happens. But there's no need to go out of your way to be a dick."

"What's doing?" asks Eric. He's suddenly appeared by my shoulder.

"We were just heading back to meet you."

He looks over at Callum and his friend, who are back to playing with their swords. Owen backs up a few steps. Lena touches the horse gently with her crop, but suddenly the grey seems determined to back up all the way to the showjumping arena, to safety, and retreats rather than advances. The horse is afraid, and Callum has no respect for the animal's fear.

"Look," says Eric to Callum. "I think you need to put your weapons down." Suddenly, Eric is in teacher mode. It's a turn-on, I admit, from the usual shambling persona he adopts when he's doing anything horse-related. His shyness, when he's not a hundred percent sure of himself, is the aspect of his personality I like least. "You're a performer; you should respect other performers."

Callum turns, roars, and thrusts his sword at his partner. Owen skittles sideways, Lena in tow.

Suddenly, Eric picks up one of Callum's spare swords on the ground. "Lay on!" he cries, brandishing its silver, and starts clanking it against the metal of Callum's weapon.

In stupefied silence, I watch my boyfriend expertly maneuver Callum out of Owen's path. "Hurry," I say to both women.

"Eric! What are you doing?" Rose is dumbstruck at the change.

"I know he's got some stage fighting certification from his days in theater," I say.

"But it's two against one! This isn't pretend!" says Rose.

Lena is still trying to get Owen to take a step forward.

"The swords are blunt, so I don't think Eric can behead Callum," I say. What a shame.

Callum is bearing down upon on my boyfriend one minute; suddenly, he's running past into nothing, faked out by Eric's phantom parry. Callum trips and falls. Sam, the bulkier friend he was practicing with, is now—less enthusiastically—taking on Eric.

I'm dumbfounded because my boyfriend appears to be winning a goddamned sword fight against two jousters. I've always been the one ready for a fight, not Eric. Eric's not drawing blood, of course, but just keeping the other swordsmen in motion, not letting up, slowly maneuvering them away from the horses. He's not winning through the dumb strength I use when fighting, but through skill and sheer endurance. He just won't quit.

"Go, go, back to the trailer," I say to Lena. Slowly, hesitantly, with Lena encouraging and threatening, Owen edges past, starts walking, perhaps even a little too fast, but Lena matches him, stride by leggy stride.

"Look, enough," says Sam. He asks Eric, "What do you want?"

"I want you to stay away from the cross-country field when you're practicing, or any place where horses are warming up or competing."

"Fine, we'll go over there, near the woods. C'mon, Callum."

Callum lingers for a moment, as if weighing his professional duty to go on with the show and his personal commitment to being an asshole, but eventually he follows his friend. A little too hesitantly for my liking, but he follows.

"Thanks," I say to Eric, genuinely surprised.

"A truly gallant knight never gloats," says Eric and bows. He's flushed pink.

"A knight brandishing a sword has never rescued me before!"

"If you challenge anyone on horseback, you're on your own."

I squeeze his shoulder. I'm more impressed than I can let on at this moment. He doesn't shrug off my hand.

By the time we've rejoined Lena, she's already untacked Owen and is ready for her cross-country course walk. But she's not alone. "Dr. Roberts!" Her uncle has arrived wearing jeans, a red shirt with white piping that looks like something from the Western pleasure ring, and is escorting two immaculately groomed long-haired dachshunds on matching red leads. They immediately start barking when they see new people coming over, creating a protective, very low fortress around their owner.

"Beverly and Wyatt?" I ask. I squat down, way down, to dachshund level. What I assume is Wyatt turns up his belly and I rub it. Beverly thumps her tail and continues to bark, looking slightly confused if she should seem friendly or fierce. They're cute, but if they were my barn dogs, I'm sure I'd be tripping over them half the day.

Dr. Roberts crates the dachshunds in the back of his Toyota RAV4. "This is my farm truck, as you can see by the bag of chicken feed," he says, rather proudly. The upholstery of the vehicle is immaculate, free of both dog hair and hayseed. He's set the feed bag upon a neatly folded towel.

Eric waits with Owen and Finnegan, who are resting in their respective trailers. He sits on an unfolded canvas chair with his Kindle. On the course walk with Rose and Lena, I point out the flags for their levels—black on a yellow background for Beginner Novice, and white on a green background for Preliminary—noting that it's important not to forget the colors of your level. "Like some people," I say.

"Simon's just throwing shade because I once got eliminated when I had a brain fart and accidentally jumped the wrong fence."

"I'm not throwing shade at you, Rose, because you went off-course, I'm throwing shade because you fell off going over a lower-level fence. You could have at least had the decency to go off-course and fall off going over something the next level up."

I turn to Lena. "The purpose of Beginner Novice, your level, is just to introduce different eventing questions—which is what we call jumping combinations—to the rider. Owen won't have a problem with any of this, just keep your leg on."

She nods.

"Are you okay?" Rose walks a little ahead of us, uncomfortable with Lena's sudden depressive funk. That's the one thing that's not acceptable in eventing.

"Just hoping I don't make a fool of myself in front of you *and* my uncle, now."

"A video of a really spectacular fall might get more hits than one of your cousin's reels putting on mascara. But if you get dirty, there's no way your uncle is giving you a ride to Urgent Care in his sterile SUV."

She gives me The Look.

I sit down on her next jump, a little table, and pat beside me. "Lena, you took two nasty spills pretty close to one another. You're coming back after a pretty severe injury. It's normal to be a little nervous."

She joins me on my perch. "But you're never nervous. I haven't been through what you've been through."

"I'm not normal. Don't be like me. I'm an idiot."

"I can't imagine what you must think."

"Well, it's not the dentist. Although Morrissey did once step on my hand after throwing me off like I was some kind of fucking scarf."

"I meant Freddie."

"Ah, I see." Lena's talking about Freddie Whitechapel, the upper-level rider I used to ride for, the rider who pulled me back to the sport when I too was thinking of quitting, long ago.

Freddie died in an accident, a rotational fall going over a table jump very much like the one I'm sitting on right now (although much larger). The horse toppled right over the jump, crushing Freddie. It was just one of those things, everyone said, neither the fault of horse nor rider. In fact, Freddie had ridden clear over the course on his previous mount.

"Lena, although I think it's unlikely that you're going to have a serious fall on this little course, if you're scared, you're scared. It may be true you haven't lost someone to the sport, but we all have our own struggles other people can't really understand unless they've lived them." I think of Lena and Paula, and how desperately Lena tried to prove herself. How so many people have needled and needled away at Lena's confidence over the years, despite her skills and commitment.

"There doesn't seem to be any in-between for me. I'm not like my uncle. I'm all or nothing when it comes to horses. Today, I'm all in."

Back at the trailer, Rose has a moment of panic when she realizes she doesn't know how to fasten her brand-new safety airbag vest to her saddle. If she falls, the fastener breaks and activates the bags. Lena's just wearing a standard safety vest she borrowed from my tack room, the same one she used riding at the horse park.

I can't figure it out how Rose's new vest works either, which annoys me, as I feel I should know everything about horses, despite repeated evidence that I don't. I'm enraged at this ridiculous, unnecessarily complicated armor, and at Rose for not trying out a new piece of equipment before a competition.

"Why didn't you just wear your old vest?"

"This one, with air canisters, is supposed to be safer. This is my first Preliminary!"

"Safer, because you'll probably miss your start time and never get to ride out there."

"I thought you had one just like this!"

"I have one that blows up with airbag canisters, but not this particular brand." Details, details.

Fortunately, the rider in the trailer next to us in the parking lot reveals she also wears the contraption and generously helps Rose get strapped in and hooked up.

Lena says, "I once put on a new pair of horse boots backwards because someone deliberately told me the *wrong* way."

"More fool you for listening to one of your hunter-jumper snakes in the grass."

"Luckily, Ainsley stopped me before I entered the ring."

Ah, Ainsley. Why does she insist on surprising us all, being a decent human being on random occasions?

Sir Eric, my knight in shining jeans and a t-shirt wipes snot from Finnegan's nostrils. "Have a good ride," he says to Rose. He's picked up on the fact that's the way to send off any eventer into the ultimate unknown of a cross-country course, versus saying "break a leg," like in acting. Even the simplest course on a trusted mount may hold some nasty surprises.

"How are your teeth?" Dr. Roberts asks me.

"The stitches all dissolved. I don't even think about them anymore."

"It's good Lena brought you in," he says. He looks at the bag of barbeque potato chips I'm holding to shove in my mouth at the next spare minute. "You need to take care of some of the other stuff I told you about. Go to your regular dentist to have a serious conversation about the beginnings of periodontal disease and your bruxism."

"My what?"

"Stop eating all that sugar!"

"Potato chips aren't sugar!"

"They're junk."

"Potatoes are a vegetable!"

"You need to get fitted for a night guard. Once a grinder, always a grinder."

I'm not wearing protective gear just to sleep. It's bad enough I have to wear it riding. "I'll get a night guard when you wear a helmet," I say.

"I have been wearing the helmet! Even my dogs have better oral hygiene than you. I brush their teeth every day," he says, picking up Wyatt to show me the tiny dog's flawlessly pink gums and white canines. "They've never lost a tooth, even though small dogs are prone to dental decay. They know the value of preventative care." Wyatt and Beverly wag their tails in unison. Dr. Roberts gives them each a baby carrot to gnaw on from a tiny little Tupperware container he's stashed in his pocket.

At the buzzer, Finnegan canters off slowly, almost like a carousel pony. His palomino color, and the fact Rose's cross-country colors are yellow and purple, intensifies the resemblance. I'm not a pony person, but admit it's a relief to see Rose having a positive ride. Moving up to Preliminary is a big jump. I know she's ready; the two of us have worked together for years. Her goal isn't to be competitive, just to complete.

As expected, Finnegan goes clear jumping, but has time penalties, putting Rose in the middle of a competitive leaderboard.

Next thing I know, it's Lena in the start box. The buzzer blares, and Owen canters over the first small house, speeds up to the next log, and I lose sight of the pair. At the Beginner Novice level, you can get time faults for going under time, which Owen looks like he very well might, but I'm not too worried, because his shift to a gallop between combinations is reasonably controlled. Lena has him back in hand to an extended canter before the next fence.

"Loose dog!" I hear. Goddamn it, some horse people have a very impressionistic view of leashing requirements. Then, with a new level of horror, I see it's Wyatt, red lead trailing after him. He's darting after Lena as fast as his little legs can scamper, barking at Owen's heels. Of course, he's barking. Just has to remind us all he's a dachshund.

I spy Dr. Roberts and Eric threading through the crowd. The dentist is holding his other dog in his arms.

"Who should I yell at?" I ask.

"Wyatt bolted when I was taking him out of his crate."

"So much for preventative care," I mutter.

I look over at Owen, who doesn't care that he's being pursued by a small, persistent sausage.

"Why did you bring Bev?"

"I was hoping if Wyatt saw Beverly he'd quit and come."

Eric, my dentist, and me run by the white rope like idiots, calling to Wyatt loudly enough for the dog to hear, but hopefully not so loud to distract Lena.

Suddenly inspired, I rattle my potato chip bag. "Wyatt! Wyatt!" He stops, torn between his desire for food and his desire to be difficult, which is something I find quite relatable.

Eventually, the dog's stomach takes control of his brain. He trots over and I sprinkle the chips in front of him. Wyatt thumps his tail and starts wolfing them down. Beverly squirms out of the doctor's grasp and starts eating them, too.

"You are an extremely bad dog," the doctor says to Wyatt. Wyatt pauses to thump his tail, then goes back to eating.

"I guess junk food has some uses," I say.

"I wonder if he's gotten overheated," he says, ignoring me. "You know raw potatoes are toxic for dogs."

"The bag says they're cooked." So am I, after today. "I just hope Lena doesn't murder me," I say.

"Why?"

"Let's just say Owen hasn't been a 'Take This Horse to McDonald's'-style mount recently."

"Could have fooled me," he says, cleaning his glasses on his cowboy shirt. "He looked pretty steady out there. But you never know with horses, do you?"

"No, you don't."

"English," he says, shaking his head. "Maybe someday she'll learn to really ride."

As I watch Owen's slate grey tail fading into nothingness, his steady, measured canter, I remember what I said to Lena. It takes a good horse to get your nerve back, after it's been taken away by a bad one. Sometimes the bad horse and the good horse are the same horse, on the same day.

Chapter 8
As the World Turns

Lena and I ride back to the barn, together, in the trailer. Eric speeds along next to us in his car. Rose hit the road with Finnegan before the prize-giving. I'll give her the brown tenth place ribbon for her Preliminary-level placing next time she lessons with me.

The air is mild, but not soggy. My mood is improving by the minute. Lena and I need to have a talk. "Well, you came in second at Beginner Novice. Your uncle's dogs got some exercise and barbeque potato chips. A successful first horse trial for you."

"I guess?"

"Lena, I hope you don't mind, but you know Owen has been for sale for a while. Ever since it's was clear that he wasn't fit to run at Advanced. I bought him for Phillip, and well, that didn't work out. Thanks to his performance with you, I just sold him."

Lena does a double take. "I can't blame you, because I wasn't planning on buying him. But how did *my* Beginner Novice ride get Owen sold?"

"Someone took one look at him loping around, chased by a barking dog, and thought he'd be ideal to bring her kid up to the next level. I think the match is decent, and I explained Owen wasn't completely without some quirks."

I remember thinking of how I'd privately worried only a strong man like Phillip could ride the grey horse, especially after Owen reared at the LARP. I guess I was wrong.

"I don't want this to be the end of our working relationship, though. If you haven't found a position you're interested in, I'd love to have you work and ride for me during the year before you go to college."

"Simon, I'm not an eventer. I had a lot of fun today. But my heart is in the showjumping arena. There is something about speeding around over those high fences that satisfies some need in me. I'm missing it even now. This very second."

I don't ask how she's going to cope with college with that urge in her heart. "Ainsley's not an eventer, and she worked for Sandra Black. I could learn from you as a showjumper. So could my horses. I promise to let you eat at regular intervals, pay you on time, and not leave for Germany randomly without warning."

"How could I refuse such an offer?"

The rest of our journey home is uneventful. We unload Owen, and I check on the other horses. Molly has fed everyone earlier, turned out or stabled (as needed) the entire barn, and appropriately shielded every horse with fly boots, masks, and sheets.

Reeking of chemical fly spray and medicinal liniment after tucking Owen in for the night, Lena and I ride together over to Eric's. His parents have invited us for dinner and he's already waiting. I meet Ms. Vandermark at the door. She looks shifty, nervous.

"Hello, Simon. Lena's mother, Ms. Serena St. Claire has arrived."

I look over at Lena. "What's going on? Is this some surprise party I don't know about?"

"I texted I was having dinner here. I didn't invite her to show up! She apparently invited herself. She does that, sometimes."

I enter the living room, which is very beige and nondescript. Except for Serena St. Claire. She's wearing a royal blue pantsuit, has a close cloud of dark curls perfectly sculpted around her skull, her makeup is subtle yet flawless (despite the heat). She's looking as if she's ready to shoot her next take.

Serena rises. "I understand you took my daughter eventing, Mr. O' Shaughnessy."

"Mama, don't blame Simon."

"Lena, you promised me you'd be careful!"

"I'm a grown woman!"

"A grown woman living in my apartment until she can apply to college."

"Uncle Russell was there at the horse trial."

"My brother probably just fouled things up and made worse trouble!"

I can't deny that, exactly. I'm trying to think of a way to break their uncomfortable mother-daughter stare-down when my phone lights up. A rider's phone ringing after a long day away cannot be good news.

"Simon O' Shaughnessy! You poached my student." Admittedly, I didn't expect Ainsley Ashcroft-calling-level bad news.

"I did what?" I put my phone on speaker so I can have witnesses in case I'm accused of more crimes.

"Now Gretchen says she wants to event. She says she's leaving Fletch's operation and wants to board with you."

"This is the first I've heard of it. Wait." I haven't checked my emails or texts all day. I scroll through my business account. "Oh. Ainsley, you can't deny that speedy little pony is probably better suited for eventing."

"I knew it!"

"I am Serena St. Claire, Lena's mother. Who is speaking on the phone? Are you an eventer?"

"Ainsley Ashcroft, and I am a hunter trainer and I ride in the ring like a sensible human being," says Ainsley, loudly. "Eventing is one of the most dangerous horse sports in the world and I don't encourage people to do it."

"You groomed for an eventer!" I interrupt.

"Who is now hiding from the tax man in another country! Y'all are crazy!"

"You see, even this rider thinks eventing is one of the most dangerous horse sports," says Ms. St. Claire, reasonably.

"I placed second in my first eventing competition ever. I helped Simon sell his horse," says Lena.

"This is Ainsley Ashcroft and don't believe a word Simon says, or Lena, who he has obviously brainwashed," blares my phone.

"What are you talking about?" I ask.

"Wait a minute, I remember you, from when I watched Lena as a junior. You rode that beautiful grey horse. What was his name, Vanity Fair? I always remembered him because his name sounded like the magazine," says Serena.

"They did a story on Mama in *Vanity Fair*, years ago," explains Lena.

"Yes, I rode Vanity Fair! Van was the horse of a lifetime. I won everything on him. No one could touch us in the hunter derbies." Ainsley's voice has softened. "I loved that horse. I still dream about him. He's retired now."

"Why can't you ride like that, Lena? On nice, slow horses."

"You don't want to know the exciting things they do to keep the horses looking so calm," I mutter, but no one is paying attention to me.

"Actually, Fletch has been looking for another assistant trainer to work with our jumper riders. You know, the amateurs and juniors. It's a riding position, too, not just on the ground. The pay's decent."

"Really?" asks Lena. She turns to me. "Simon, this is my dream job."

140

"I thought you were studying for your SATs," says her mother.

"I thought you were thinking of grooming and riding for me!" I say.

"But there's still a year before I go off to college." Lena turns to me. "This is showjumping, doing what I really love. Simon, didn't you say that after Paula, I needed to start putting myself first?"

"Not like this! You stole my employee!" I say to my traitorous phone.

"You stole my client, fair's fair," says Ainsley. "And her little pony, too."

"I know this is probably a very inappropriate time to bring this up, but Ms. St. Claire, I have listened to every cast album you have ever recorded a million times since I was a teenager," interrupts Eric.

I kind of freeze up at what strikes me at the freakish inappropriateness of his comment. I mean, this woman is famous, so she must hear fawning compliments all the time, right?

But Serena laughs. "Thank you," she says. "If you ever have a piano handy, I'll let you know what I sound like in person."

"Oh, I've seen you on stage and in concert—several times. But we do! Have a piano, I mean," says Eric. "In the next room." He hesitates, then makes his way over to the instrument.

I cringe in embarrassment for him. But I realize Serena isn't upset. In fact, she looks rather eager as she follows him.

Ainsley has hung up. Eric sits down at the keyboard. "I teach drama at a local high school. I often have to play accompaniment." For once he sounds proud of what he does, not ashamed. He's talking and running through scales, as easily as I can talk on my cellphone and warmup a horse.

"Do you know 'Unexpected Song'?"

Eric plays, with no other prompting, and Serena sings. I'm shocked, because the pure, vulnerable voice that pours forth from her body is so different from the imperious, brusque persona I see on screen, or even her rather tightly contained self in the everyday world.

As she sings, she seems to relax. The music comforts her, more than my words, more than any reassurance I've been able to give her Lena's going to be okay. Eric's accompaniment is fluid, following her voice as it speeds and slows.

Suddenly, imperceptibly, something happens in the room. A relaxation of the tension that existed there before. Eric's parents sit and watch their son play for the celebrity in our midst. I'm surprised Eric isn't more nervous, given that under the best of circumstances, he can be clumsy and unsure of himself.

But I remember how when he's teaching in a classroom, all his shyness ebbs way. Serena has flicked a switch of confidence, one I always hoped would be turned on by horses. His voice is deeper, he's suggesting songs from shows I haven't heard of, he's comparing different covers of these Broadway songs and standards he knows so well.

It feels like five minutes ago Serena was accusing me of risking the life of her daughter. Now, she's sitting on the couch with Eric, saying, "I remember when I had my first Broadway audition. The man waited for me to finish and said, 'Miss St. Claire, I have a list of songs I tell people never, never to use for an audition. 'If I Loved You' is number one.' I was mortified."

"Brutal! Oh my God, how could you have known?" asks Eric.

"Needless to say, I did not get the job. However, I did play Julie Jordan many years later, so revenge is perhaps best served cold, like a fine white wine." For emphasis, she sips the chilled Chablis that Eric's parents have provided. Ms. Vandermark looks as proud as if Eric's going to marry Serena, at this point. I'm feeling a little left out. We haven't had a real dinner, but are eating cheese, salami, crackers, and drinking wine, which suits me fine at this point (though I'd prefer beer).

"Why don't the writers on your soap write you a singing scene?" I ask.

She makes a sweeping gesture with a cracker studded with a hunk of cheddar, and proclaims, "It's supposedly not *in character*." She eats the Ritz.

After Lena and her mother have left, I linger with Eric on the front steps of his house. Although his parents appeared to have defrosted a bit towards me, I still don't feel totally at ease in their presence.

"I'm more impressed by how you calmed down Lena's mom than the swordplay."

He bows. "I'm sorry you lost Lena to Ainsley."

"It's okay. I promise not to make you pick up the slack at the barn when Molly goes into full bridezilla mode."

"When she gets divorced, I'll be happy to offer advice," he says.

"You hopeless romantic, you."

He kisses me. He's never done that without looking over his shoulder for his parents. He can tell I'm a little taken aback. "I like to use an element of surprise in my attacks," he says.

Chapter 9
Ainsley Again

Two weeks after the horse trial, Gretchen and Rabbit Rabbit move in and Owen moves out. One grey in, one grey out, which seems fitting and right in the grand scheme of things. My first eventing horse Fortune's Fool was a grey, and I've never been without at least one in my barn for long.

When Owen walked into the trailer, to be shipped south to Pennsylvania, to the land of Eagles fans that burn rage into my Patriots-loyal heart, I thought I saw the ghost of my ex standing next to him in the trailer, talking in his low, even, and gentle voice, as he always did to horses—and often to me, unless I really angered him. Sometimes I still miss that voice, if not the man. But just as quickly, the swing of the hay net near Owen's soft sable nose flicked that spirit into dust.

Ainsley calls me as I watch Rabbit Rabbit bounce around the field. I turned him out in a small paddock alone, but hopefully he can partner with one or two geldings as he acclimates. "How is the Malloy pony you stole from me?"

"Still alive after a day at an eventing barn," I say. "As is his rider. I've found it bad for business to kill too many of my students, right away."

"That's not even funny, Simon."

"It's not, which is why I resent your insinuation that I treat my horses and riders like crash test dummies," I say.

"You did Lena."

"I did not! I got her confidence back, and you're reaping the benefits."

I watch the pony throw himself onto his back and grind green grass into his light turnout sheet. "I'm not making it easy to get dirty, am I, Mr. Rabbit?" I slap a mosquito on my arm. The bugs are wicked today. Fall can't come soon enough. I may choose to run my operation in Maryland for its closeness to Kentucky and Tryon, but my loyalties will always lie with the bitter bright autumn leaves and stinging winters of New England. "How is Lena doing?"

"We just got back from the Paradise Ridge showgrounds."

It's Monday, so that sounds about right. Fletch's barn is away almost every weekend at some show. "Wow, you put her right to work."

"You have no idea. I feel like I've been through the Maclay or a marathon or something. I have some epic gossip for you, Simon. Epic!"

"Make it quick."

"I can't. You need to sit down and listen."

I sigh. "I always used SparkNotes in high school, and I don't see any reason to change. If this is going to be a long story, I'll pass. I've gotta go."

Molly leads Morrissey from the paddock to his stall for His Majesty's supper. She closes the door before he can rush past her and drag her into the stall, then slides open the door again and leads him in, once she's forced him to pause in a mannerly fashion. As soon as he's released and the latch has clicked closed, he kicks the door hard, and slams his bucket against the wall, before dunking his muzzle in the grain. He knows she's won this round. He can concede defeat, but I never can.

Chapter 10
Ainsley Ashcroft Explains it All

Since Simon won't let me tell Lena's story properly, I, Ainsley Ashcroft, am going to have to take over. Strap in.

So, Lena and I are setting up and helping the grooms bed the stalls at the Paradise Ridge showgrounds, and suddenly I hear *that voice*. I look over at Lena.

"I thought Paula was in Suck-cla this summer." I throw another forkful of fragrant cedar shavings down.

"Paula never shows in Ocala," says Lena, voice tight.

"What, she thinks it's beneath her?"

Lena goes back to fluffing the bedding. Paradise Ridge has really nice stabling—brand new, with perfectly level floor mats. "She'll hear you, Ainsley."

I thought I smelled Paula even before I heard her. The stench of cheap Chardonnay, desperation, and Sore-No-More.

"Maybe I should have stayed with Simon after all. At least I know I won't run into Paula around him."

I gently poke Lena's skinny ass with my plastic purple pitchfork. She jumps out of the way.

"If you were at Simon's, you'd be eating at a garbage food truck in the middle of a field, tacking up his horse tied to a trailer near a puddle." Our forks still have all their spokes intact. Fletch runs a high-class operation that way. "Let's grab doughnuts and regroup. The doughnuts are the whole point of coming to Paradise Ridge this early."

Duck Duck Dough—the Paradise Ridge doughnut vendor—makes its jam, cinnamon, and cream doughnuts al from scratch. If I were still working for Sandra, I'd be running around looking for oat milk in a wasteland of foul burger trucks, so she could blend whatever packet of protein powder was currently sponsoring her. "I'm an athlete and I eat like one," she'd say. Glad I don't have to hear that anymore. Here, I can relax like the civilized human horse person I am, living the Dover catalog of my childhood dreams. If I wanted to be an athlete, not a rider, I'd be in friggin' gym class.

I am back where I belong, I think, gouging out the filling of my half-eaten blueberry-filled powdered doughnut with my tongue. The seating area near the horseshoe circle of fancy food trucks has cushioned chairs so soft I could lie back and take a nap on one of them. I've specifically chosen a table on the outskirts in case Paula comes here to eat. I need to survey all the riders at rest, all our competition.

I don't just mean riding competition. I need to keep an eye out for any hot, up-and-coming international riders who occasionally flit through Paradise Ridge. Along with fruity pastries, those guys are my greatest weakness. Phillip wasn't foreign, but he spoke French and several other languages, which is practically the same thing.

I'm relieved to be here, half-drunk on the smell of new saddle leather from the vendors and the sight of people walking around in polished boots. I raise my coffee and clink Lena's white paper cup. "To glamor, grooms, doughnuts, and no more checking my weather app a million times to see if my rider's going to be paddling through a flash flood on course."

"I'm not gloating until our riders survive the warmup ring." Lena doesn't seem to have Sandra Black's obsession with protein, despite her skinniness; she's gotten a hot cinnamon sugar doughnut drizzled with dulce de la leche with her coffee. But she's sipping and nibbling nervously. She's one of those people who loses her appetite when she's stressed. If she wasn't so nice, I'd hate her for that alone.

"Our riders will be fine."

Lena looks at me meaningfully. She brushes the sugar from her long fingers onto her napkin.

"They'll be fine," I say, "because we're going to ride the horses in the warmup ring first, before they even think of getting on."

Our two junior riders, Tori and Anna, haven't been showing that much at this level. They're both in lower-level divisions. In the warmup, Lena rides Tori's Brashfull, a gentle 17.2h bay gelding with a Black Beauty-like star on his forehead. As I'm barely above five feet in my tall boot stockings, I'm chosen to ride Anna's Melodious Dancer, a 15h strawberry roan I privately think looks like My Little Pony because he's slightly pink.

I'm not sure where she found this horse. It's not Fletch's doing. She bought him before she moved to his barn. Mel's sound and jumps over anything that's put in front of him, but my hunter's eye disapproves of anything that's not bay, chestnut, or grey. I swear the gelding's got Quarter Horse hidden in that muscular behind of his. Oh well, this is still the junior jumpers. Even on the A-circuit, what can you expect? I'm sure Lena's uncle would love him.

I'm so jealous of Lena, how her long skinny legs just drape around Brashfull. I've often ridden horses that big, but I look like a stubby little child with my stirrups adjusted correctly. Lena is weaving through the sea of horses, elegantly mounted as a queen. Juniors and amateurs who blindly obey their trainers are piloting the rest of the horses in the ring, screaming "diagonal line" and barreling through whoever is in their way. You'd think these people were on the *Titanic* heading for the last lifeboats the way they steer themselves to the practice jumps under the stink eyes of their trainers.

Paula is, apparently, not only beneath going to Ocala but also beneath getting on her student's horse to school him.

Instead, she's thrown her rider—an amateur I vaguely recognize named Florence Bauer—like a sacrifice, into the center of the warmup. I'd never do that. I take care of my riders, my meal tickets, even though no one took care of me, ever, when I was learning the rules of surviving an A-circuit warmup, back in my days of braids and jodhpurs.

You can hear Paula shouting at Florence, above everyone else. I haven't taken single a fence on Mel. Mel knows how to jump, and the best thing is to keep the horse calm and compliant, as I lengthen and shorten his stride, avoiding all traffic. It's like pole-weaving the Incompetents out here. At least Mel's Western Quarter Horse breeding is good for something.

I give Paula a good, hard look. She's a sturdy block of a woman with her hair pulled back in a tight braid that's a scratchy mix of sun-bleached blonde, bleach-bleached blonde, and grey. Squinting in the sun at out-of-shape middle-aged women's legs sliding back over jumps has given her eyes a permanently crinkled appearance. She always looks angry, which gives her an air of confidence some amateurs and juniors mistake for knowing what the hell she's doing. Not all trainers are nasty to cover up the fact they can't quite figure out how to teach, but many are.

Paula isn't clueless; she had a decent enough career as a junior rider and then got lucky, finding work as a trainer at a respectable barn. I'm told back then she worked like a dog. She rode in Europe for a few years, made some connections, and gained a reputation for importing horses cheaply, putting juniors on them, and winning enough ribbons to keep well-heeled parents happy.

But even at her best, she was always barking out the same instructions, again and again, to her riders, and bitting a horse up rather than stepping him down to prevent his rider from being over-faced. There were whispers her best students and her fancy imported horses were the ones making her look good, rather than the other way around. In the middle of all this mess, she got married and divorced, and picked up a habit of drinking white wine from a water bottle all day.

What does this matter in the warmup ring? I just have to be careful not to crash into any of the riders flying like popcorn around me.

Florence is one of the most dynamic pieces of popcorn. She's a woman with wispy blonde hair under a hairnet a shade too dark. Her rigid shoulders are almost immobile, markedly tense even compared with the others in the ring, mostly other stiff-armed amateurs or juniors with braced, jammed-down heels.

Florence robotically obeys Paula's command to go for the oxer in the center of arena and ends up nearly running into Lena's horse. Lena immediately and expertly steers Brashfull away. She avoids a collision but Florence's horse spooks and launches his rider to the ground.

Florence Bauer's horse Fly by Day, a very orange chestnut gelding (a more garish shade than Simon's Morrisey), is now galloping around the circumference of the arena. For a half a second, I'm thinking Lena is going to put her uncle's cow-rustling skills to work, but no. The horse slows down after a lap, stops, snorts, and then waits for someone to grab him. Paula does the honors, coward that she is, only after it's clear the horse's little tantrum is at an end.

Florence has to be carried out of the ring by the EMTs. She's apologizing furiously to the medics, although they seem rather relieved someone has broken herself, to break up their dull day. They go into full concussion assessment mode on the sidelines.

"Don't ride your courses like that lady on the stretcher," I say to Tori and Anna, who have been watching this entire performance, ashen, from outside the arena.

"Um, okay?" says Tori.

Ah, ambulances, nice if you can afford them. With no insurance, if I get hurt, I end up driving myself to Urgent Care. I'm surprised at Paula, though. She's almost acting like she cares, the way she's bent next to Florence.

Tori's best ribbon is fifth, but every round in her division she's clear with no time or jumping faults. Anna's Melodious Dancer pins ninth twice, which might be a little bit my fault for not urging her to go faster and or to leave out more strides. I'm so used to coaching hunters. Oh well, at least she didn't fall off. Paula's braying at the warmup ring made all of us other trainers look nicer in comparison, which might be her greatest gift to our sport.

When we're packing up to leave, since none of our riders are in any of the evening classes, what to my wondering eyes doth appear but Florence Bauer's chestnut Fly. He's now braided and mounted by junior, heading into the warmup ring for the Child/Amateur Owner Classic. It's one of the more prestigious amateur classes of the day. There's even significant prize money for the winner.

I can't resist. I go over to Paula. "If he wins any money, Lena deserves a cut for taking your rider out. I'm assuming his owner signed off on you paying for a braider and paying a pricey entry fee for the Classic."

"He needs to be schooled. He needs to learn he can't get out of work by being naughty," Paula says, rather smugly.

I haven't been back on the A-circuit for long, so Paula has apparently mistaken me for someone who believes her bullshit. "Fly doesn't need to be schooled. He was just doing what his rider was telling him to do. It was your rider who

152

steered him into Lena. If he needs schooling now, you could just as easily ride him yourself in the warmup ring, without charging your rider an extra fee for the Classic."

Paula glares at me and takes a big swig of her bottle of mint iced tea, a clear yellow beverage that bears a conveniently similar appearance to white wine.

"But this way, you get to charge one of your juniors for riding him, and get his owner to pay the fees for braiding and showing, right? As part of his 'training.' Does your rider know you entered a horse in a class with such an expensive entry fee?" I ask.

"Of course!"

"Where is his rider?"

"In the hospital. And it's none of your business."

"I guess it's none of my business either that even a basic wine bitch like myself can smell the vanilla and oak of bad Chardonnay from that iced tea bottle?"

I find Lena to tell her. She is, of course, surprised yet not surprised in her low-key Lena way.

The next day, we note on the online schedule Paula is now going to be riding the same horse in the open jumpers, a pro class.

"I assume his owner, lying in a bed in the hospital, knows she's paying the entry fee for this class as well?" I say.

"Can you spare me for a few hours?" asks Lena.

"Why?"

"Because I'm going to tell Florence Bauer what Paula is doing."

"No, you have to wait until my pony kid's done with her division. I'm going with you to the hospital."

"Ainsley, I really should go alone."

"I can't let you do this alone, Lena."

"I don't need the favor."

"Favor! I am not letting you have this drama alone! Who do you take me for? Don't be so selfish. I live for this shit."

We convince various levels of hospital staff we're friends with the patient we're trying to see. The breeches and boots help. I get a feeling that they assume we're giving off the same crazy *eau de equine* as Florence, so we belong with her.

We introduce ourselves to Florence, saying we work for Fletcher Cox. Florence seems pretty out of it. Her memory of crashing into Lena is foggy. "I thought Paula just said she was going to school Fly in the warmup, so he didn't have a negative experience showing?"

"She had one of her juniors ride him in last night's Classic, and she's planning on riding him herself today," says Lena.

"Oh, I'm sure you're mistaken. Maybe she's riding him in one of those ticketed warmup classes, where you pay a fee to school some jumps, so the ring won't be so crowded. I get so confused by those busy rings. I was just riding him in a few amateur-owner classes. He'd need to be braided and everything for a Classic."

"She had him braided!" I blurt out.

"Wait—what?" Florence pulls herself up. Her voice is no longer soft and slightly slurred. "Paula had my horse braided?"

Lena and I both nod.

"Paying for a braider? I don't understand. He didn't need to be braided for my division, the amateur jumpers. Braiding!" Like many wealthy people, she doesn't mind spending large amounts of money for questionable reasons—like being encouraged to show a horse she can barely stay on in a crowded warmup—but she's furious about being blatantly cheated out of relatively tiny sums. I've been in the horse biz all my life, and still can't figure it out.

154

"I can't wait to see what my bill is going to look like, with the braiding and entry fee for the Classic." Florence sinks back onto the stiff hospital pillow. She jerks up her head. "Did he win anything last night?"

"He was third, so he won some prize money," says Lena.

"Paula didn't even text me. Did she think I wouldn't say anything when I saw the results posted online? I'm exhausted just thinking of fighting the bill. What can I do?"

"Move your horse to a different barn!" says Lena.

"But I bought Fly from Paula. I've always ridden with her." She goes on about how she's not sure Fly will adjust to a new environment.

I tune her out. For a rider, I haven't stayed in many hospitals, but this one is dire. When I was visiting a friend in Wellington who fell off during a Grand Prix, she was in a private room with paintings and an enormous television. Of course, she had great insurance through her job. Here, there's nothing but a thin puke green shower curtain surrounding us, and the nurse is hovering, looking antsy, clearly itching for us to leave and take the smell of horse and our mucky shoes with us.

Oh well, the showgrounds at Paradise Ridge are relatively new. I'm sure after a couple of years some healthcare company will build something nice for all the riders that break themselves in the arena.

Florence is no longer in her breeches, but Lena and I are, and even our driving moccasins and exposed tall boot socks are pretty fragrant in the antiseptic room.

Florence is still talking. "I admit I've wondered about those bills for supplements I wasn't sure Fly needed. She did her training rides on him during all those odd hours when she knew I was at the office. I kept planning on showing up unexpectedly, but I was afraid she'd get angry. Plus, things have been so crazy at work."

"She was probably using him in her lessons with other students. Charging the rider for the lesson on a schoolmaster and charging you for training. I used to be one of her working students. I saw all the things she pulled. I didn't even understand it was wrong," says Lena.

"What do you do for a living?" I ask Florence, because I'm curious.

"I'm an attorney."

Wow, that takes balls on Paula's part, to screw over a lawyer. I'm more impressed by the minute.

Florence continues, "Horses are my relaxation. I put Fly in full training so I didn't have to be the one making difficult decisions about my horse."

"Okay, I'm making the difficult decision," I say. "Ms. Bauer, you need to get up from that hospital bed and get Paula off of your horse."

Riding in the back of Lena's Toyota with her foot propped up on a pile of folded saddle pads, Florence sounds a bit more chipper than she did in the hospital bed. "You must think I'm a terrible fool. Paula said she thought Fly was the perfect horse for me. But he's been more than I can manage on my own. I get tense, then he gets tense, and then he spooks, and I get more tense. Or I get overwhelmed and forget my course, or turn into someone in the warmup ring, like I did with you. It must be hard for you to understand. You're young and not afraid of anything."

"Lena's evented. She's, like, superhuman."

Florence looks shocked, even though Lena assures her that the eventing she did was pretty low key. That seems to make Florence even more in awe of Lena.

"But you had that terrible fall, and look at you, back and riding like nothing ever happened."

"That's one possible way to sum up the past year of my life, sure," says Lena.

We speed through the showgrounds on Fletch's's golfcart. Florence is getting her energy back. Or the painkillers are wearing off, but the adrenaline of being about to confront Paula is kicking in. I can feel the attorney surfacing within her.

She goes off to speak with Paula in private, but I can only make out a few words here and there. First, there's tense, angry whispering. Then, I hear Paula offering to help electric tape Florence's tall boots onto her swollen leg, so Florence can ride Fly instead of Paula today.

"Don't do it," I pray through gritted teeth. Then the two women get too quiet for us to hear.

"We shouldn't be listening," whispers Lena. She grabs my arm and steers me to the concession stand. Like Paula deserves privacy to hang herself by her own rope, backpedaling like mad.

"God, I hate a shitty braid job. Did you see the one on Fly? Paula didn't even find a decent braider."

Lena sits down and puts her head in her hands. I order a coffee. Lena shakes her head without looking up when I ask if she wants anything. I sit and read my phone to pass the time, sipping sweet milky caffeinated goodness. "Let me guess, you're a Libra. Your horoscope will give me a clue how this will play out."

"I'm not really into astrology."

"Tell me, Lena! Tell me! Don't be like Simon and give me that 'astrology is beneath me' routine. You want to know."

"Libra. And I don't care, for reals."

"Typical Libra. Likes to be in control."

Florence hitches a ride on someone's golfcart with her crutches and zips over to tell Lena and me to lead Fly to Fletch's stabling area. He's going home with us. Paula's not riding him in the pro division after all. She's already spoken to our boss.

We have to get through Paula, who is blocking Fly's stall door. I don't know what she's playing at. The horse doesn't belong to her. Unless Paula is delusional enough at this stage of her career that actually believes whoever can ride a horse best owns said horse.

"You," she says, pointing at Lena. "You did this to me."

Paula is stone-cold sober. I will say, for a functioning alcoholic, she remains very good at rationing her functioning days for the really important moments. I guess she really thought she had a chance of winning something on Fly.

"You did this to yourself, Paula," says Lena.

"After all I did for you!"

"Making me work for no salary? Not coaching me at shows, even though my mom was paying you a training fee?"

"Don't nickel and dime me, that's not how this industry works."

"Paula, if you can pay to compete at this level, you should be able to get real help, not a kid! My mom isn't rich, just because she's an actress. It was feast-or-famine for the two of us. You knew she was desperate to do anything to keep me on a horse, because I was begging her to let me keep showing. If I did anything wrong, it was lying to her about all the shady stuff I saw and making her feel guilty. You knew how desperate I was to fit in."

"What does that mean? What kind of card are you playing?"

"I don't play cards, Paula. I'm just saying facts are facts, you saw a kid who would have done anything for you, and done anything to keep riding and showing, and you took advantage of me."

"I haven't had everything handed to me on a silver platter like you have!"

"You. Handed. The. Care. Of. Your. Whole. Barn. To. A. Teenager."

"I would have been grateful for that at your age!" Paula's eyes are ablaze with fury, through the cracks of her sunburnt crinkles.

"Then you charged my mother for the privilege of her child running the barn! I'm just proud all the horses got fed and nothing got burned down."

"You're a quitter, Lena. I always said you were. You quit on me, and you quit on Pilot."

Silence.

I hear Lena swallow. Painfully. "If quitting someone who was hurting me makes me a quitter, fine, I'm a quitter."

"You rode some very nice horses," adds Paula, as Lena barrels by her with Fly. Paula is still bristling, but it's like she's shrunk an inch or two, and Lena's tall frame has stretched.

Without looking back, Lena says, "I will give you that. They were all better horses than you deserved." I watch Fly's tail swish. The cheap thread on the braid is already unraveling.

Chapter 11
Simon Again

"You're bumped up higher on the waiting list for the family reunion, Simon," Lena says to me the next time we talk on the phone. I'm on Morrissey, warming him up by strolling around the perimeter of my property. It's getting light later. Fall is coming, I can feel it in the thickness of the horses' coats when I brush them, and the crisp morning if not the midday temperatures. I give my horse a slightly longer rein than usual, to stretch his neck. But not too long.

"I didn't do anything special," I say.

"My mother is in love with your boyfriend. Watch him carefully when she's around."

"Watch your back. Ainsley will steal your man while she smiles and smiles."

"As long as she doesn't tell me to put my horse's boots on the wrong way. I'm only here at Fletch's for a year. Still studying for my SATs."

"Sure. Just like I'm giving up sugar and flossing away," I say.

"I checked on Pilot," she blurts out. "I called that dressage rider who bought him."

"Is she still alive?" I ask.

"Pilot jumped out of the ring during his first dressage show. But it's much harder to unseat a rider crashing into a little white plastic fence an inch or two high. So yes, she's still breathing."

"Good news!" I return my attention to schooling my crooked horse after saying goodbye.

I circle Morrissey before the first jump of the stadium course I've set up. Morrissey sails over the jump easily, and my release with him is automatic, soft, fluid. For once, Morrissey hasn't clipped the first warmup fence, and the rest of the course remains up as well. *People don't change,* I tell myself, as I canter 'round the arena, to remind myself not to believe, not to hope. I told myself not to believe in the possibility of change when I finally pushed Phillip away after he flitted back and forth from me and from horses.

I dismount, raise the rails, and remount.

Now I really feel Morrissey's muscular surge beneath my thighs as he clears something of appreciable size. His jump is powerful, agile, and tidier than it was at the beginning of summer. As the joys of riding a confident mount surge through me, I can cleanse my heart of memories. I'm no longer riding a horse who threw me, who refused at ditches, who tried to buck me off. I've even briefly forgotten the more recent past, the rank nipping at me when I curried his dirt-encrusted hair before I rode. I exist in the moment, stride to stride, no grudges or expectations.

Part of me knows this sense of oneness will quickly fizzle out, like the beauty of the light illuminating Morrissey's shining ginger coat will quickly dim in the shadows of the barn. Just like the connection of making love with a man surely ends. I let myself savor what lasts, this perfect centaur-like fusion of horse and human.

I finish at the barn midmorning. Molly is in charge for the rest of the day. I shower and find myself outside of Eric's door, a surprise visit which half surprises me. His mother answers. She's still in her bathrobe. Her glasses are pale pink and unflatteringly large, rather than the horn-rimmed geek chic style her son has adopted. She's soft and rather shapeless; her form is wholly unlike what Eric has crafted his own body into with his daily, punishing running.

162

"Eric's still out pounding the pavement. It's his long run day today," she says. I'd forgotten. Maybe he won't want to go out with me if he's tired after running ten (or more) miles.

There's an uncomfortable tension as I sit on the couch. "Would you like some breakfast?" his mother asks. Unlike my mom, she has an internal social script to smooth things out between people. In contrast, when my brother Sean was foolish enough to bring a date to our house, Mom would ignore the girl and just start talking about colic, founder, or sheath-cleaning. Legitimately, because they are subjects that come up with horse people, but also as a test.

I was in such a rush, I didn't make my planned McDonald's stop. Ms. Vandermark comes in with a tray bearing coffee, a glass of grape juice (something I haven't seen since snack time in kindergarten), and buttered rye toast. I remember how when I first met Eric he served me a snack of coffee and cookies, and I now I know from whom he gets his manners and his myopia. I apologize for coming so early.

"Oh, it's ten in the morning; it's my fault for not being dressed. I'm sorry we're out of milk."

"I'm sorry I'm out of interesting celebrities to bring along with me for show-and-tell." I don't drink coffee normally, but I'm tired and I sip its black bitterness out of politeness and to clear my mind.

"That was something! Serena St. Claire! Eric is still buzzing. I haven't gotten over it myself. I've always loved musicals. Frank," she says, referring to Eric's father, "is always telling us both to turn our music down." Just like her son, she has classical music playing in the background, soothing stuff, rather than the melancholy notes Eric puts on to grade essays and brood.

I'm getting a sense that Eric's father thinks musicals are the reason there's a gangly six-foot man on the family sofa right now, rather than a petite blonde soprano.

"Frank and I were so worried about Eric. I know *you* know Eric went through a bad time as a teenager. After his marriage to his *husband* didn't work out and he came back to live with us, I worried some more. He seems happier now."

"Thank you. I'm happy, too," I say. I sense she's trying. The word *husband* sounded like she wrested it from her throat.

Eric's parents never outright stood in the way of Eric dating men. They accepted him back into their home after what he not-so-affectionately calls his starter marriage failed. Yet when he was younger, they sent him to an orienteering camp for kids with mental health issues. The supposed reason was to heal his depression. What half-closeted gay kid isn't depressed, now and then? Instead of fixing him, he fell off a camp horse, lost even more confidence in himself, and was miserable not being able to act and sing. They set Eric up to fail at a place where only sports had value.

The fact his parents sent him away, it's easy to read between the lines. While they don't reject their gay, musical and Shakespeare-loving, dramatic son, it would have been easier to accept a straight one. Sometimes I wonder if Eric's insistence upon not being extraordinary, of admitting he was tired of being judged as an actor, of refusing to make up for his failure to meet his parents' expectations of heterosexuality, is even braver than my insistence I excel, day in and day out.

Perhaps Eric and I are good for one another. I have always believed as a trainer that you need to leave the horse better off than how he was before. It's why I gave Morrissey to Phillip for a time, because I was afraid I'd ruin him. It's why I always try to end a schooling session with Morrissey

164

now on a positive note, even if it means resisting my competitive nature and resorting to the simplest of exercises. That my teaching might make a human being better, that's harder to believe. Especially a human who doesn't ride.

"I hope the toast isn't too crunchy! I poured you grape rather than orange because the cranberry grape is lower in sugar."

"Eric's filled you in on my tooth situation, I guess."

"What a surprise it was, when Eric started dating someone horsey! Eric's always been afraid of animals, especially horses."

"Believe me, I know," I say.

"He's never been physically brave. But he'll get up on that stage and sing and play the piano for hours, no matter what the size of the crowd. Oh, here's Eric."

"Simon! What are you doing here?" Eric's in shorts and a sweat-stained light blue t-shirt that proclaims **Come From Away**.

"Don't worry, she didn't reveal any big secrets or show me any embarrassing high school photos," I say.

"I never went to my prom, so she's limited," he says. His glasses are foggy with sweat. Pink and panting, he looks like he's in a different climate zone than Ms. Vandermark and myself, who have been sitting still in an air-conditioned room.

"I checked the website and the Maryland Renaissance Festival is still selling tickets at the door today. I wanted to know if you'd come with me. I know you have school stuff, but I figured on the weekends during the summer, you'd be free."

"Simon! Going to another Faire with me, that isn't necessary."

"Well, it wasn't necessary to save my—to help me out with Callum and then with Lena's mom, but you did it." I look over at his mom. I still don't have a reading on her likely reaction to the phrase *saved my ass*.

"Let me shower. I'm so hot and sore from running right now, I can't think," he says.

I finish my breakfast under Ms. Vandermark's supervision. Eric returns in jeans and a Sisters of Mercy t-shirt. We match, sort of, in faded back t-shirts and jeans, and he follows me outside.

"I approve of the t-shirt."

"Unlike you, I'm all over the place in my musical tastes."

"I have a one-track punk-alternative mind."

"Don't you have to tend to the horses today?"

"I rode Morrissey this morning. Molly will handle the rest. Get in the car, loser."

"You're the loser, you're with me," he says, lingering on the sidewalk, before sliding into the passenger seat. I give his shoulder a squeeze before speeding off.

"Eric, stop that. I don't like to hear you say that, not seriously."

"I just feel weird when you come over and have to pass through the gatekeeping of my mom."

"She makes great toast."

"She does. Next time you stop over, you'll have to try her cinnamon raisin variety."

"I guess that's why you haven't moved in with me. I don't even bother to toast my Pop Tarts, half the time."

"Simon, we've been through this before."

"You said you needed to be on your own for a spell after the divorce. I hoped that spell had passed."

I ease the car up to a gentle eighty on the highway. Eric opens the window, letting the rush of air inside into our space, and I do the same, to balance the pressure on either side of the car.

"I'm just not sure I fit into your life. If you wouldn't be happier with someone else more horsey."

"Do you have any suggestions?" I turn up the music. "Joe Strummer is dead, Brandon Flowers is married to a woman, and you've been number three for some time."

"Since you saw my sword-fighting skills?"

"Absolutely. Way better than me fighting with pitchforks against my brother when we mucked stalls."

"My stage combat certificate doesn't cover pitchforks. You see, we can never work."

"Yes, we can, Eric. If you want it to."

"I do," he says.

Both of us listen to the wind roar. The highway is uncrowded, mercifully, so I can go as fast as I want, without worrying about some Maryland driver driving in my blind spot. Every driver has blind spots.

"The last time I was in a serious relationship, I messed it all up."

"I'm not asking you to marry me, just move in with me." I think of my barn manager Molly pouring over the Bed, Bath, & Beyond website to set up her wedding registry, dreaming of a home filled with dishwasher-safe plates and a man who wants her to quit a job that requires her to live at the barn. "Just to move in and let me make us toast now and then. I'll let you be you, and you'll let me be me, okay?"

At least, Eric's chipped mismatched mugs have images from Broadway musicals or Shakespeare plays. He's nothing like me, but I feel at ease with him.

I slow the car ever so slightly. "You know, when I was fourteen, I used to drive illegally all the time. Mom knew. In fact, she taught me. It was helpful when we had to pick up hay or grain and she couldn't get off work. I never got caught."

Unlike my grain and hay deliveries as a kid, my speed right now has no purpose other than to feel joy with another man. With Eric beside me, the feel of motion vibrating in my hands through the wheel and the wind flattening my hair, I feel perfectly alive and content. I'm half-forgetting what I have lost, where I am going, and where I have been.

THE END

About the Author

Mary Pagones is the author of the popular Fortune's Fool equestrian fiction series. She is also the author of two YA novels—*Pride, Prejudice, and Personal Statements* and *The Horse is Never Wrong*—as well as the mystery novel *A Study in Scarlet Marquis: Sherlock Holmes and the Trials of Oscar Wilde*.

A graduate of Wesleyan University and Harvard Divinity School, and the veteran of many creative writing workshops (including Annie Dillard's, Amy Bloom's, and Jill McCorkle's), she makes her home in New Jersey. She lived for two years in the United Kingdom, in Birmingham and London.

Mary's Social Media Links

Facebook:
https://www.facebook.com/Mary-Pagones-Author-106178421345656
Twitter:
https://twitter.com/marypagones
Instagram:
https://www.instagram.com/pagones721/
Email:
pagones721@gmail.com